Succulents and Spells

ANDI R. CHRISTOPHER

Copyright

Contents

Succulents and Spells

Laurel ignored the knock at the door. Any time before ten was too early to expect a witch to interact with the world, in her opinion. She'd been working in the cafe until late last night, and had just finished her coffee and twisted her blue hair up under her shower cap, ready for a hot shower. She shivered as she stepped out of her dressing gown. She'd done a lot to make this flat habitable, but nothing could ease the July chill of an old flat on the sunless side of Aro Valley, pressed against the damp hillside.

Twenty minutes later Laurel was warmed and clean and the bathroom smelled of her cousin's homemade lavender and thyme soap. She pulled on her jeans and a thick brown knitted jersey and pulled open the curtains. Days off were terribly rare lately, but this time she'd turned off her phone.

The sky was a bright winter blue and the breeze gentle. She was going to have a good day today. Her flatmates were at work, and she had the house to herself.

In the hallway, she stopped to check on her succulents, on top of a bookcase beneath the window. They were doing surprisingly well - healthy-looking and thick with moisture. Maybe her life was a mess in other ways, but at least she could keep a plant or two alive.

Turning to the kitchen, something caught her eye. She turned back and looked out of the window. There was someone there, sitting on the crumbling brick wall between her pots of marjoram and lemon balm. They seemed quite happy there, in a purple t-shirt despite the cold, and their hair buzzcut to almost nothing, tapping their Doc Martens against the wall.

Laurel opened the door and used her best customer service voice. "Can I help you?" she asked. So much politer than *what the fuck are you doing here*?

Looking up, the person on the wall scrambled to their feet. "Hello, my name is Marigold Nightfield, and I'm here to ask if I may please have some tissue samples from your monster."

Laurel sighed. All hopes for a straightforward day had just gone out of the window.

"You'd better come in," she said, clearing a load of clothes off one of the wooden chairs by the dining table, which was cramped against the kitchen wall. She hadn't been brought up to turn magic folk away; hospitality was – sometimes annoyingly – how her family worked. "I've just had the last of this morning's coffee, but would you like some tea?"

"I only really drink liquorice and fennel or lemongrass and ginger. But just hot water is fine too."

Laurel stood on tiptoe and began searching through the alarming number of half-used boxes of teabags. She checked the expiry date before offering – excellent adulting.

"This one's liquorice and star anise. Is that close enough?"

"Lovely, thank you."

Laurel stuck with peppermint for herself, then cleared a boardgame and a stack of books from the opposite chair, and sat down.

"So, let's start this again, shall we? Who did you say you were?"

Marigold took a deep breath. "My name is Marigold Ann Nightfield. I use she/her pronouns. I'm a PhD candidate in biomedical science."

Laurel offered her hand across the table, and Marigold took it.

"Laurel Windflower. She/her as well." She didn't mention the incomplete MA she'd been postponing, for one reason or another, for the past two years. "So, is your PhD in monster biology or something?"

Marigold shook her head. Tibbs, Laurel's one-eyed, torn-eared, statistically-should-have-died-a-decade-ago cat, was sniffing around her boots. Laurel told people he was her pet, because even those who knew about witchcraft could get a bit weird about the word *familiar*. Marigold reached down to stroke him, and he didn't object.

"Not exactly. I'm doing a personal research project as well. And I'm trying to collect samples from as many monsters as I can, and because you're so close, I was hoping you would let—"

"It's up to the monster really. He sort of does his own thing. I assume most monsters do. Can't say I've ever made the acquaintance of another."

"But you *are* a witch?"

Laurel nodded. "Yes. Not a very interesting one, I'm afraid. They rented me this room because they thought I'd be cool with the monster. Which I guess I am, but I don't really know anything about him."

She took a long sip of her tea. She'd had to couch surf well into her second year of undergrad, before she'd found this place. The guy who was moving out wasn't from a family Laurel knew, but he'd recognised her name and knew she was a witch. She didn't see anything wrong with getting a room because of it; the market was abysmal for renters and plenty of people got a room because they could pay extra, or they owned a fridge, or because their parents knew someone. Being a witch was sometimes an advantage, but it wasn't an unfair one compared to all that.

And she had done the place plenty of good. Bit by bit her spells had vanquished the mould from the walls, and dried out the rooms, so the windows didn't leak all the time. The property manager was receptive to their requests for maintenance, and if he had any thoughts of raising the rent they disappeared as soon as he crossed the front doorway. Laurel didn't usually like nudging people's minds like that, but property managers – like Work and Income caseworkers – were an ethical exception.

The monster made some noises in the night but was otherwise no trouble. Most of the time he stayed below the floor.

"Have you seen it?" Marigold asked.

"Only from the other end of the hallway... he's pink with yellow spots, kinda furry, and according to my former flatmate, he's called Alfred."

"Alfred?"

"I'm sure it's not his chosen name. But it's weird to have someone in the flat you just call *the monster*, I suppose. A bit dehumanising. Even if he's not human. Anyway, anyway backtrack. You're doing a PhD? How *old* are you?"

It was a blunt question, but Laurel felt that when someone bangs on your door before ten in the morning, asking to take tissue samples from your monster, they've lost the right to all niceties. And besides, she *had* given Marigold tea.

"I'll be twenty-four in November. I know I come across young. It's because I'm autistic, and enthusiastic about things, and also because of my skin."

Laurel leaned forward, just enough to catch the scent she was expecting. "Geranium," she said, "and chamomile."

"Picked at the half-moon," confirmed Marigold. "Because you want a subtle potency, not your skin torn off. I probably started it too young, and it makes me look like a kid. Still, no acne ever! My grandmother was a witch, but my dad and I are both only children, and neither of us have magic. Probably the line will die with me. But it doesn't mean she couldn't teach me things."

Laurel smiled, despite herself. "It works, doesn't it?"

"It does." There was a pause. "So, is it okay, if Alfred doesn't have a problem with it, if I take some samples of tissue?"

"Will it injure him?"

"It's just like a big needle I use. He'll feel it, but it's not like I'm cutting him open or anything."

Laurel wanted to say that this was a ridiculous idea and usher this strange woman out of the house immediately. But right now, she couldn't think of a single good reason why, if Alfred didn't object, she should stand in Marigold's way.

Which is how it happened, that she ended up holding a stranger by the ankles of her Doc Martens boots, as said stranger stretched down the hole in the back of her wardrobe headfirst, with a syringe in her hand, talking to a monster in gentle tones.

The monster growled. The two of them went back and forth like that for a while – Marigold shuffling her body in the wardrobe, Laurel gripping her ankles.

"Got it. Pull me up, please." Then Marigold said something that was unintelligible but sounded a little like a thank you.

"Could you understand him?" Laurel asked, as Marigold dusted off her jeans.

"Random fact about me: I was born with the ability to talk to monsters."

"But you're not a witch?"

"Nope. It's not magic, it's just... heightened processing and perception and stuff. My grandmother tested me through all the usual. I can put together a basic potion, just because I've practised enough times, but there's not a spark of magic in me, much as she'd have liked there to be."

It sounded a lot like magic to Laurel, but she wasn't going to argue with someone about their own abilities.

Later in the day, when she was stretched out on the sofa eating fish and chips with her flatmate, Connor, and feeding pieces of squid ring to Tibbs, Laurel heard a low growl from below the floor. Her ears pricked up, suddenly anxious, but then the growl settled into a contented purr, low and rumbling beneath her. Alfred may not have liked the needle, but perhaps he didn't entirely object to seeing a new face once in a while.

\#

In Wellington, you know you will bump into everyone again at some point, but Laurel heard from Marigold just three days later.

Laurel was tired. She'd worked a morning shift through until after lunch, after a late shift the night before, with not enough sleep in between. Her feet ached and so did her shoulders, just from carrying things back and forth. The endless list of variations of a flat white still hung in her head. She felt like she was working all the time but, at barely above minimum wage, it was only just enough. The last bit of the walk home seemed impossibly steep, even though it wasn't far.

Not for the first time lately, she thought about how her life was going nowhere. Her sister was a legislation witch working as an accountant. She said legislation was much more important to accounting than numbers, though Laurel couldn't see how. Her (non-magical) brother had achieved his dream of becoming a Department of Conservation ranger. They were not alone. Laurel came from a big family, where everyone of her generation seemed to have found their niche, magical or not. Except her. A half-completed linguistics master's, that she wasn't likely to be getting back to any time soon, a room in a cold student flat, and a poorly paying hospo job. Sure, things could be worse, but it didn't stem the ever-present sense of failure that seemed to cling to her.

Up the hill at last, and she checked the mailbox. Along with the bank statements for people who hadn't lived there in years, and a power bill, there was a package with her name on it. Hand-delivered. And it smelled good. Curious, she took it inside with her, putting the power bill on the fridge before opening the package. Inside was a small plastic container, like the ones Chinese food came in, and a note on a post-it. *Thank you for letting me talk to Alfred x Marigold.* And then a phone number.

She opened the container to find four pieces of thick gingerbread, the soft sort, like cake. Instantly, smells flooded her senses; ginger and cinnamon, soft butter, smells of old kitchens, smells of home. It wasn't quite her grandfather's recipe, but it was close enough. Laurel wondered if their ancestors had crossed paths; maybe they'd exchanged recipes or spells hidden in a barn or deep in a forest.

She saved the note on a blank page at the end of her spellbook. The volume wasn't her family's original spellbook, the one with the leather cover and an impossible combination lock that could only be operated by the mind. That had gone to Alyssa, a master of algebraic witchcraft now living in Canada. But she'd scanned it page by page, so the rest of the cousins would have a copy. Laurel had printed it off and pasted the spells into a sketchbook with some of her own notes, and she'd pressed herbs between the pages until it started to smell a little like the original.

There wasn't anything earth-shattering in there. People with pre-conceptions about witches would be surprised to find it full of herb poultices for headaches, and hot drinks to clear the mind before making important decisions, and nothing at all about turning people into frogs. That sort of herbalism wasn't all there was to witching, not by a long way, but the book was important to Laurel, in part, because it had been handed down through generations of her family.

She found herself strangely perked up by the gingerbread, whether it was something in the recipe or just the nice surprise. Perked up enough to make a proper dinner even. A quick text to her flatmates, to check they'd be home, and then she was making enough lasagne for three with leftovers for lunch, putting garlic bread in the oven, and clearing the table and chairs enough so all of them could sit down at once.

Connor was the first home, eyeing the garlic bread, but Laurel was strict.

"Proper meal tonight, and we're waiting until Leilani gets home," she told him

Leilani had just landed her first professional job – a policy analyst role – and was trying to make a good impression by not heading out of the door at five. Laurel had some opinions about that, but had decided not to share.

She thought, as she served up the meal, that at least she was living with people she liked. She'd known Connor half her life, and Leilani just a year or so, but the vibe of the flat was right. Messy, maybe, but not gross. People paid the rent and mostly cleaned up after themselves. No dramas. Everyone was chill about the monster. And sometimes, when they were in the mood, and their schedules aligned, they'd sit down and have a meal. Like adults. Like a family.

\#

Laurel opened a pack of drawing pins and stood on a chair to hang a bag of herbs in the corner of Connor's room.

"Hey, hey, hey! Didn't the landlord say no drawing pins?"

Laurel rolled her eyes. "Also no picture hooks, no tape, no Blu-Tac—"

"Correct."

Laurel ran her hand over the wall. She'd dried it out, but it was still worn with scars of damp and mould. She could feel it in the plasterboard and through to the space where insulation could have been.

"Because he does so well at protecting this place." Laurel pushed the drawing pin in and breathed in the blend of thyme and mugwort. "Don't worry. He forgets this stuff as soon as he leaves, I make sure of it."

"We won't be here forever. If this software we're working on gets some decent investment, I'll be able to draw a salary, and then we'll get a modern apartment somewhere."

Laurel shook her head. "I won't be able to afford that."

Secretly, Laurel didn't want to move, and didn't think she could. She wanted to stop putting so much energy into the landlord's feelings, but there was her garden and Alfred, and Tibbs wouldn't be happy about being stuck in an apartment. She didn't know if Connor really realised he wasn't exactly a regular cat, and... there was history in this old weatherboard house.

"You're practically my sister, Laurel, and how many times have you spotted me for rent. We'll work something out. Just... for now I seem to be pouring time and money in..."

Laurel wanted to tell him to get some sort of job, even a stop-gap job. But she knew he struggled with having to do things in a way that didn't make sense to him. He was lucky – or privileged enough that so far, at least since they left school, he hadn't had to.

Laurel sighed and placed the bags as close to every corner of the room as possible. With her fingertips, she willed the mould to stay out of the wall.

Connor was one of the few people who knew her powers were real. She'd told him as soon as they'd become friends, back in middle school, but he'd been unconvinced until she got him through a crucial stats exam, despite him having been drinking until 3 a.m. the night before. She'd made him apologise for years of scepticism as soon as he walked out of the exam room. That was the precise moment she'd stopped taking Connor's bullshit, and their friendship had been stronger for it ever since.

"Thanks, Laurel," he said, moving to the edge of the broken sofa excitedly. "Want to see what I did get today?"

"Go on," Laurel said.

Between his habit of going through skips, a freecycle group, and the occasional op-shop, Connor accumulated an alarming amount of stuff at minimal expense. The room was something of a shrine to it, though Laurel had resolved to stop it taking over the rest of the flat.

"So, I got that bread maker over there," he said, and then, when Laurel turned to look, he pulled something from behind his back. "And this!"

"What the fuck?" Laurel said, looking at what appeared to be a large metal hand, held in her direction.

"Go on, shake it!" He put on a cartoonish voice. "Good to meet you, Laurel."

"I'm not shaking your trash. What is it?"

Connor placed it on one of the upturned crates that served as bedside tables. It was a slightly larger than life-size model of a human hand.

"I think it's some sort of palmistry model. Look, it shows the lines and has things written on it, like wealth and..." he squinted "...love."

"And why would you acquire something like this?" Laurel asked, rolling her eyes but not entirely surprised.

"Okay, so I was thinking if the whole accounting software thing doesn't work out, we could collaborate on something. An app where you scan in your palm and it tells your fortune. My business and coding skills, your witchcraft... What do you say? We could make our millions together."

"Connor, have you ever, in the more than ten years you have known me, seen me read a palm?"

"It's not like I'm spying on you."

"I'm pretty sure it's not real, Con. And if it is, it's not something any witch I know does. How would it even work?" Laurel sat down beside him, trying not to fall into the cavity left by broken springs at the edge of the mattress. "Still, our own business would be nice."

"We'd rule the world! Hey, work that bad, is it?"

"Kinda."

"I'm sorry."

"No, it's okay." Laurel shook her head. "I mean, it *is* okay. It's not the worst job I've had. I don't get yelled at. They pay me on time."

"Low bar there."

"Yeah, well, I've worked in hospo a long time. It's not bad, I'm just exhausted. One shift after another, and I never seem to catch a break, and if I do get a day off, I end up spending it catching up on laundry because I'm too tired the rest of the time."

Connor put his arm round her. "Capitalism's shitty, Laurel. It's shitty to us all."

"Says the entrepreneur," Laurel said, without enthusiasm for the teasing, leaning her head against him.

"If you can't beat them..."

"Hmmm. Hey, but I did meet someone the other day." Laurel stood up and went looking, unsuccessfully, for beer.

"*Meet someone* meet someone?"

"I dunno. Probably not."

"Okay, this is sounding interesting. Walk and sushi?"

"Yeah, sure. Let me get my shoes on."

They ate sushi on wooden chairs outside the shop, bundled up in the cold, though the sun was pushing through. Laurel told Connor about the strange young woman, who somehow knew about the monster in their flat, and had come to take samples.

"You totally like her."

"I doubt I'll ever see her again. She'll be off doing her sciency thing."

"Have you looked her up on Facebook or anything? Hey, if she's a PhD student she'll have a university email."

"No need. She put her phone number in with the ginger-bread."

Connor got to his feet in mock outrage. "Her phone number? Laurel Windflower, you're seriously telling me she gave you her *phone number* and you don't know if she's interested in you?"

Laurel could feel herself blushing. "Enough."

For once, to his credit, Connor took the hint and didn't mention Marigold Ann Nightfield again the whole walk home.

\#

"They're looking good," said Leilani, as Laurel moved her succulents around on the bench, trying to make the most of the small glimpses of sun the flat got at this time of year.

"Thanks," she replied.

They did look surprisingly good. Laurel had collected succulents since her teens, loving the thick, hardy leaves, and the way so many of them grew out in geometric patterns. Her mother had called her "green-thumbed" but she'd never had a knack like that with other plants – and she'd tried, just in case she was some kind of gardening witch. She kept her herbs alive, but you'd have to be actively trying to kill it to make Italian parsley go away. Same with mint. The more delicate ones took some effort, but she mostly made it work and had enough relatives around the place who could give her cuttings when the worst happened.

But her succulents were plump and healthy and evenly coloured, even though they shouldn't handle the low temperatures all that well. Laurel had thought about taking the landlord to court over the new insulation laws, but then she thought about what would happen if anyone tried to install underfloor insulation in a space occupied by a large, furry, yellow and pink monster and decided better of it.

"Hey, I'm going to the supermarket. Do you need anything?"

"No, thanks. But I think we're low on laundry powder."

"Already on my list."

Leilani was just out of uni but already proving herself a good flatmate, Laurel thought. She looked at the Topsy-Turvy with its heart-shaped leaves. She'd want to repot that before spring. Otherwise, they wouldn't need much care – wouldn't even need watering until winter was over. She glanced at her phone. She'd need to get changed and head off soon to make it to the lunch shift.

Her phone buzzed with a message on the family witch chat. Which sounded more exciting than it was – just a group chat of almost all the witches in the family. One cousin needed some comfrey urgently, but before she could reply, an uncle who was closer had already offered to help out. They were a weird family, even by witching family standards, and big, with what Laurel suspected was a higher than average inheritance of magical powers. The ultra-specific arguments about spells, sometimes with heavy doses of passive aggression, got annoying sometimes, but at least it meant Laurel was never entirely on her own.

She gave a thumbs-up sign to the chat, then pulled on her black pants and shirt, brushed her hair, and, with her phone in her pocket, walked out for another day at work.

\#

The next day, Laurel was sitting on her bed, trying to hand-repair a tote bag. She closed her eyes and willed the fibres to part around the needle, the stitches to find themselves even, muttering a crafting charm under her breath.

A stab of pain as the needle went straight into her finger, a spot of blood. She yelped, sucked her finger, and proceeded to finish off the bag unevenly by sheer force. Fuck the weave parting for the needle; the only way she was going to get there was by stabbing it.

Laurel was no fibre witch. No craft suited her; the disastrously wonky results of last year's community ed. pottery class, and however many years of knitting, with her cousins forced to help her pick up dropped stitches all over the place, made that abundantly clear.

"Someone's at the door for you," Leilani said, poking her head into the room.

Laurel got up and followed her through to the kitchen, where a young man she didn't recognise was waiting.

"Connor said you could give me something to help me sleep that worked." He was tapping his hand against his leg nervously, not making eye contact.

Laurel privately wanted to kill Connor, but this kid wasn't at fault and he looked pretty close to the edge right now, so she wasn't going to take it out on him.

"What did you have in mind?" she asked, keeping the door open only a crack.

The man shuffled his feet. "Just like, the doctor wouldn't give me anything. Said to have warm milk and... and a guided meditation podcast. I'm lactose intolerant and..."

"So, you were hoping I could get you prescription drugs?"

"Well, uh, Connor said..."

"Connor knows full well I don't do that sort of thing."

"I'm sorry to have troubled you."

Laurel opened the door. "Hey, don't go. I can help you, but it will be... alternative, I suppose you'd call it. Are you on other medication? Any allergies?"

The man shook his head.

"And when you say you can't sleep, what do you mean?"

"Just that I'm so stressed about everything. It goes round and round, and I'm so worked up I can't sleep."

Laurel sure as hell wasn't inviting a second stranger into the house, and she didn't particularly want him sitting on the wall either. She was only doing this because he was clearly in a state and she felt bad for him, and she'd read so many articles about depression and suicide epidemics lately that she never wanted to risk being someone's last straw.

"Come back in two hours, okay?"

As soon as he left, Laurel lit the gas stove and placed her iron pot atop it with just enough water to stop it burning through. Then, she grabbed her trowel and in the garden dug up a clump of valerian. Saving the leaves to dry later, she cleaned the root carefully and added it to the pot, with a little more water and adjusting the temperature until it simmered. Main ingredient sorted.

The moment her back was turned, Tibbs was up on the counter, getting dangerously close to the pot. She lifted him down and chucked him outside. Valerian root smells like catnip – she should have remembered that one.

Retrieving her secateurs from where they had fallen down between the fridge and the wall, Laurel headed outside again – while keeping an eye on Tibbs, because he was crafty even by cat standards – to cut some lavender. She added it to the pot along with more water and some vodka. Then, she held her hands above the potion and focused all her energy: on sleep, on restfulness, until she could almost feel it travel from her fingertips into the mixture. That was what distinguished it from something any herbalist could make. Still, it was a simple spell that didn't require too much energy.

When it had simmered sufficiently, she let it cool and then strained it into a glass bottle which had once held lemon cordial. She wrote out some brief instructions and a simple two-line spell – a general wellbeing one she felt like she'd known since she was an infant.

"What do I owe you?" the young man asked, when he came to pick it up.

"No charge for my services. But a small koha for the ingredients is appreciated if you can?"

The young man thanked Laurel nervously, promising to give some cash to Connor to pass on, and thankfully left without further discussion.

Laurel slid a note under Connor's door: *You're an asshole.*

Then she texted Marigold:

>> *Thank you for the gingerbread! It was delicious.*

#

The Uber dropped Laurel on a winding street in Wilton, in front of a house that was all geometric shapes of glass and concrete, which must have been fantastically expensive even by Wellington house price standards. She turned her head and there were the sort of views of the harbour that could only be described as magnificent. When she'd taken Marigold up on her invitation to see her lab, and see the use Alfred's biological samples were being put to, she wasn't expecting anything like this.

"Hey!" Marigold emerged from the side of the house.

Laurel felt something uncomfortable as she got out of the car, a sort of shudder running across her skin. She dismissed it, even as her heartbeat seemed to grow louder. Just nerves.

"Is this your house?" she asked Marigold, incredulously.

"It's my dad's. He's in India for the year on some sort of architecture fellowship. I came back from Dunedin about the time he left, so it made sense for me to housesit for a year. Take care of the cats and the garden. I guess when he comes back... I've been reading a lot of articles about adult children living with their parents, and apparently it depends on whether you can approach the relationship differently or get stuck in the old patterns. So, we'll see if we work as flatmates. It's a bit silly having all this space just for him."

Laurel felt that a dozen people could probably live in a building this size and not get cramped, but she kept that thought to herself. She felt like all her muscles were shuddering beneath her skin, or perhaps as if there was a heavy bass being played somewhere, and she was feeling the vibrations through her flesh. She swallowed and walked into the garden.

It was the opposite of the house; old fashioned, well-tended, but a little wild in its own way. It was the sort of garden Laurel hoped to one day have. Every type of herb she knew, and a few she didn't, which was unusual. And thoughtfully planted – companions next to each other and some of the plants ordered by common uses. A perfect mixture of scents, that gradually changed as she walked through.

"Did you plant this?" she asked.

"My grandmother. She lived here from not long after I was born, until she died a couple of years ago. I take care of it."

"It's a perfect witch's garden. I reckon she'd be proud of how you've kept it up."

Marigold hunched her shoulders up around her face. "Thank you. I have timed sprinklers set up on the home automation system, which helps. If there's anything you don't have, you're welcome to take cuttings."

"I may take you up on that. Is your lab in here too?"

"It's downstairs. It's not like a fancy lab or anything. But it's enough to work on the projects I can't do at uni."

Laurel followed Marigold down the steep pathway at the side of the house, to the lowest level, and through a small door. The house was built into the hillside, so this large room only had one window, near the door, but it was brightly lit. It was fitted with a white melamine bench on one side and metal tables covered in equipment Laurel couldn't name. Some of it looked more like machinery, others like cutting or pinching instruments.

"So, this is my lab," Marigold said, grabbing a desk chair. "Have a seat."

While Marigold perched on a stool, Laurel wondered what the fuck she was doing accepting an invitation to someone's lab. She was pretty sure she'd seen movies about this, and they didn't end well. I mean, sure Marigold was smart, and cute, and not only chill about the witch thing (which not everyone was) but knowledgeable about it. But *come see my underground lab* did have something of the supervillain about it.

"So, what are you researching," Laurel asked, suppressing her qualms. "I mean, I know monsters but..."

"Have you ever noticed monsters well... leave bits of themselves lying around?"

"Yeah." Laurel had. She'd assumed it was just one of the ways in which they were monstrous. On his night-time roams through the flat, Albert had dropped claws, patches of fur, and long round columns that she hoped were toes. If they weren't, she really didn't want to be told otherwise. Connor refused to deal with them, which was how she'd managed to negotiate putting cleaning the toilet onto *his* chore list.

"People diverge a little genetically over time. You're determined by your parents' genetic makeup, and by a level of random mutation. But it's quite easy to define set attributes that the vast majority of people have – two legs and the like. Not everyone, but almost, yeah?"

"High school biology awakening at the back of my brain," Laurel said, scratching her head. She was still feeling uncomfortable, and she didn't think it was just nerves anymore.

"Okay, so monsters are all over the place. They can have eight legs or six tentacles or one foot like a snail. They can be any colour or pattern thereof. They can have fur or feathers or scales. There's no 'probably' or 'almost everybody' about it. If you didn't know a particular monster, you simply couldn't guess what they looked like. You follow?"

"The only monster I've met is Alfred, and I've barely seen him, but sure."

"So, there's this huge rate of mutation. If people mutated that much, it just wouldn't be survivable, but when I say things like DNA and mutation they're approximations. Monsters aren't part of the same category. They didn't evolve in the way we did."

"Good thing or bad thing?"

"Bit of both. The downside, for the monsters, is that medicine just isn't a thing. Even magic medicine. They're too different from each other. Most of the time, if something goes wrong or they're in pain, it can't be treated – you can't develop monster paracetamol because pain would work differently in every monster. And they're at the point of understanding where this is important to them."

Laurel hadn't even thought about this aspect before. Tibbs got taken to the vet, when necessary, but Alfred just had to deal. She'd never heard anything that particularly resembled pain before, but then, how would she know? She swallowed and let Marigold continue.

"The good side, for both us and monsters, is that when parts of them mutate and grow rapidly – when, in human terms, they develop tumours, which they do a lot – their bodies isolate those cells and eventually the clump of cells, whatever they are, drops off. And I'm thinking, if this is an effective way monsters deal with tumours – and they're very long-lived, so we can assume it is – could there be something in there that carries across to humans?"

"You're trying to cure cancer?" Laurel asked, incredulous for at least the second time today. Marigold's statement seemed to both make sense and be preposterous, all at once.

"Yes and no. There are too many different types of cancer for it to have a singular cure, and most new cancer treatments are more aimed at slowing down cancer or improving lifespan than they are a cure, whatever that means. But I think whatever mechanism isolates tumours in monsters could help find new ways of suppressing metastasis in humans, which is usually how cancer gets really nasty. But I'm *also* trying to find out what the actual commonalities in the make-up of monsters are. There have to be some – we're just looking in the wrong place. And once that happens, a whole system of monster medicine has the potential to be developed."

Laurel noticed Marigold's eyes shone as she started to talk about this.

"And you'll just, what, turn up to the drug companies all: *hey, I've been studying monsters?*"

Marigold laughed. "Nah. For the human stuff, there are enough people in senior positions who know about... things not commonly acknowledged. They'll help obscure how I came to my conclusions and pass it on to the right people. I won't get proper credit for it, but I'm doing my PhD so I can one day get to one of those senior positions and help with this stuff. Hopefully in a non-profit research foundation. And when it comes to monsters, well, that will have to be done off the record of course, but there are enough of us interested. Okay, so here..." Marigold got up and showed Laurel a machine in the corner. "Here's how I extract the monster equivalent of DNA."

Laurel leaned over to watch, as Marigold put a sample into a machine and adjusted the settings on the front. It whirred into motion, and Laurel caught the scent of Marigold's hair as she moved in. She could identify every herb in there, imagine them being picked from the garden outside, soaked in hot water and strained. But there was something more in among them, something that wasn't growing in either of their gardens. A scent that was just... Marigold.

"This is my tissue homogeniser..." Marigold said.

Long, scientific words like that *should* have been enough to snap Laurel back to reality, but instead she found she was smiling, enjoying every word Marigold was saying.

Get a grip, she thought to herself, but she didn't lean back. She was a witch, after all. Complicated processes and endless experiments to find the right solution was part of her world as well.

"It breaks open the rest of the cell, so you can get the DNA out. Then you use lysis, which is basically cleaning away the cellular proteins. Literally. With detergent."

Twenty minutes or so later, Laurel had a much better idea of what a whole range of equipment was for, even if she didn't think she'd ever understand how it worked – and was frankly glad she wouldn't have to. And she'd agreed to sample Marigold's latest batch of cookies.

Marigold opened the internal door to a narrow staircase, and as Laurel began walking up, what had been a background hum became a loud fast thump, seeming to shake the house and every organ in Laurel's body. She looked back, wondering if they needed to cover for an earthquake.

Marigold was walking up the stairs behind her, seemingly unaware anything was happening. Laurel swallowed, unnerved.

Up on the main floor of the house, in a large living room with a fancy kitchen, it got louder still – or at least, that was the only way to describe it, even though it wasn't sound exactly. It made Laurel nauseous. She struggled to get words out.

"I... I think I need to go," she said, propping herself up on the arm of a very comfortable looking sofa.

Marigold looked disappointed. "Oh. Are you okay? You're looking a bit pale."

"Yeah, I think I'm just sick... overwhelmed."

"I get overwhelmed a lot too. Let's get you outside."

Marigold opened the front door and Laurel practically ran into the garden, her heart beating fast. There was still the background hum, but the shuddering had stopped. Laurel found the lavender and breathed it in deeply.

"Here are some cookies for you to take. Do you need me to call you an Uber?"

"Thanks... no, thank you. I think I might walk into town and pick up some things. Get some exercise. I'm sorry to leave so suddenly."

"Seriously, it's fine. You stay safe though."

Caring too, Laurel checked off her mental list as she left the house. She regretted having to leave so quickly, and not just because it was impolite – but that house was unbearable for her. And she wasn't sure why.

#

The harbour shone a deep blue as Laurel walked down the hill, the wind in her hair. She could see the city that had come to be her home from different angles as the road curved and zigzagged down, flashes of the central city and the harbour between houses. She loved Wellington's hills, even if she didn't get up them very often, and the valleys between them, the clusters of houses and shops, the trees overhanging the pathways.

She felt calmer now she was away from the house, and a little bit silly, but it really had been unbearable. Marigold had said *she* wasn't a witch, so Laurel supposed that must be why it hadn't affected her. She'd try looking it up later, maybe ask the witch chat about it, if she could deal with their cacophony of opinions. For now, she was enjoying the walk in Wellington's characteristic wind, heading down towards the Hutt Road where the land turned to flat, and the trains ran into the city beside the port and the stadium.

Rather than heading into the city, though, Laurel turned to walk up into Thorndon. The main road mostly housed bistros and boutique shops, which she couldn't imagine being able to afford, but behind the back of an antique shop, and along a little path, there was an unassuming door. She opened it and the bell jangled. Witch Way Magical Supplies. It wasn't a secret but had no need to promote itself – those who needed it knew where to go.

Laurel raised a hand in greeting to the witch behind the counter, an older man with a thick beard. A skink – the man's familiar, she assumed, though it seemed impolite to ask – slowly made its way across the counter.

She didn't visit this place often, despite it being not too far from home. She wasn't exactly an advanced or busy witch, and she could grow most of what she needed herself. But there were some things you could only get here, and it felt like a place she belonged. So she took her time, looking at the glass jars and paper packets, seeing what was new in stock.

Some of what was sold had labels that began with *Equivalent of*. There were some witches who evaded biosecurity laws to bring in ingredients. Laurel had a dim view of them – there was plenty growing here, much of it native, and to endanger what they already had seemed antithetical to everything witchery meant to her. But she really appreciated these packets, with effective substitutes for shed snakeskins and the like. She picked up a couple of the cheaper ones, to show her support and because she knew anything might become useful one day.

She made her requests for a couple of supplies she knew she was low on: copper shavings and dried orchid petals, and the retailer carefully measured them out, calculating the total.

"Much planned?" he asked.

"Just stocking up... Hey, I don't suppose you'd have any idea why I'd sense something really loud, but not exactly a noise, that no-one else could?"

"Hmm, interesting question. Remind me, what type of witch are you again?"

The dreaded question. There wasn't exactly any rule that witches had to have a speciality, but – at least in the circles she moved in – most did, and long before they were twenty-six. For Laurel... it just hadn't happened. She'd taken a linguistics degree, thinking she might be a word witch, but even though she had a general aptitude for words, she hadn't found any kind of magical underpinning to that ability. Which had something to do with why she kept suspending her enrolment on her MA.

She wasn't going to tell the shop witch any of that though, even though he seemed like he'd probably be sympathetic.

"I'm really just focusing on herbalism for a bit," she said, hoping he wouldn't push her to admit she was still only doing the same set of fundamentals every witch in her family could do.

"And the other people who didn't notice it, they were a witch or...?"

"No. Witching family, but no magic herself."

The man spread his arms. "It could be so many things, sorry. Some kind of magical object. A lingering spell. Unlikely to be a haunting, because other people would pick up on that too. I don't think I can help you beyond that."

"It's a good start," said Laurel, scanning the noticeboard for anything of interest amid the notices of gatherings and room wanted posters. "Thanks for your help."

"Any time, come again."

The bells jangled as she left. Her precious day off was almost at an end, and already the light had begun to dim, long shadows stretching across the paths. Figuring she'd walked plenty today, so a little more wouldn't hurt, Laurel wandered through the Botanic Gardens up to Kelburn, and then down past the university, to Aro Valley and to home.

#

The next day, Laurel got home from work mid-afternoon, tired after an early start. She threw off her work clothes and got into track pants and a hoodie. She'd been feeling a little ill at ease all day, after what had happened at Marigold's house, and had had no real time to catch her breath and think about it. She made herself some soup from a packet, and some toast, and sat with her phone for a while. She hated being so awkward around people. All through high school it had been her and Connor – she had been the supposed "good influence", the one who was quiet and studied hard and volunteered in the school library; Connor had been the prankster, the schemer. Of course, it wasn't as simple as that, but close enough.

They'd never actually pretended to be dating, but they let everyone think that, or at least there was no room for anyone else in their lives but each other. Pretending they were straight when neither of them were. Shielding themselves from the inevitable gossip, or worse, of a small town. They hung out with other people, of course, and Laurel had her siblings and many cousins, but it wasn't until she left for Wellington that she actually got close to anyone. And she still felt like she blew just about every social interaction. Especially the ones that were important to her.

She texted Marigold:

>> *I'm sorry I left like that yesterday.*

The reply was almost immediate:

>> *Don't be sorry. I know I talk too much about my weird stuff.*

She was blaming herself. Exactly what Laurel didn't want to happen.

>> *No, your stuff is interesting. It was something magical that made me feel ill, I don't quite understand it yet. Can I make it up to you? Maybe coffee and cake after I finish work Thursday afternoon?*

The confirmation that came back was considerably more upbeat. Laurel smiled, put the details on her calendar, and picked up Tibbs who was stalking around the kitchen, looking annoyed about something. He settled on Laurel's lap despite himself, and let her stroke his fur. He had come to their house on the day she was born and made himself at home, which was a pretty classic sign that the baby's a witch, though it didn't always happen like that. He'd be at least twenty-six by now, and admittedly he did look old and had some bald patches on his back, but he seemed happy and otherwise healthy. Laurel fully expected him to live as long as she did.

She messaged the witch chat: *Anyone heard of a witching family called Nightfield?*

No immediate responses, but a bunch of her family were overseas, or working jobs with regular hours. She let it rest for now. If they had any information, it wasn't likely to be earth-shattering. If she was going to find out what had caused such a strong reaction, she was going to have to enlist the help of Marigold and go looking.

Alternatively, of course, she had the option of never going near there again.

She didn't want that.

\#

Laurel went through her spellbook, and a few other sources she had access to. There were a couple of things she thought might help: A Spell to Make a Malign Presence Reveal Itself was the most promising, though the guy in the shop had already ruled out haunting, and she didn't really think the "sound" was malign as such, just strong.

Still, it was worth a try. Then there were variations to find lost items – and she wondered if they could be reworked into finding an item that was causing something, even if she didn't know precisely what that item was. Finally, there was a spell for tracing witch lineage, which didn't immediately seem useful given that Marigold knew who her grandmother was, but she made notes and checked they had the ingredients anyway, because it sounded like it could be useful.

She had just about finished flipping through, when another caught her eye. A Spell to See the True Nature of a Power. It was pretty vague what that meant, but the instructions were detailed. It was a complex potion. Once made, you needed to water a plant with large leaves with it, and wait until it held the potion in its leaves. Then you had to watch at exactly the right time before it sucked up other water. If done right, an image would form on the surface of the leaves. Laurel wondered if you could just point a webcam at it, set it to record and go back to find the precise moment – Connor would help her set up something like that.

She had a thought. Succulents hold water for a long time. It wasn't the best time of year to be watering one, but she was sure she could sacrifice one to the cause if it became necessary. They would show exactly what she needed.

She'd done all the preparation she could. The only thing left was to talk to Marigold. And if things went nowhere with her, well, she could just never go back to the ridiculously expensive house in Wilton with the weird energy, or force, or whatever it was. She'd remain idly curious about it, sure, but there was no reason to think it was going to have a future impact on her life.

That would be the sensible way to imagine things going. And yet, a world in which she didn't see Marigold Nightfield again seemed impossible.

She was being ridiculous, she knew that. Marigold wasn't her type. Her previous relationships, all two of them, had been with women older than her, slicker, more professional. Definitely not the type to talk excitedly about monster experiments. And yet... and yet...

Well, one thing was planned, she was seeing Marigold tomorrow, and where it went from there, she'd just have to leave to the future.

Laurel laughed. She wasn't super into divination – and there were limits on its accuracy anyway – but she wouldn't be a witch if she left anything just to accuracy. She went to her shelf of tarot decks. Her usual was moody purples and greens, animals in gold foil, but this called for something lighter. A floral deck, flowers and herbs, painted in water-colours – much more the mood. She lit a candle for focus, and shuffled then cut the pack. It wasn't long before she had to be at work. A simple three-card spread then, face down on her purple velvet cloth.

The first card was for the past. She always disliked these the most – things she couldn't change, memories she was embarrassed by. She flipped it over to get it out of the way. Eight of cups. So, indecisive when it comes to relationships and emotions, stuck in a rut, scared to make a choice and thus going nowhere. That fitted. Enough on that. She turned over the second card.

Laurel smiled to herself. The Magician, a bearded old man, filled with power and wisdom, his staff pointing outwards, showing the way, and at his feet a purple iris, signifying wisdom. This was the ability to make things manifest, to have power and to use it, to bring about the change you wanted to see. Laurel took it as an assurance she was on the right track.

And the third card. Laurel flipped it over cautiously. Two of cups. Damn. The romance card. Or at least, the *very close connection between two people*" card. In the painting, two lovers, androgynous in their presentation – one of the reasons she'd chosen this deck – lay among wildflowers with their arms loosely around each other, enjoying nature together. She was even sure one of the flowers – with its golden yellow, curved petals – must be a marigold.

Damn. Things were seeming a little too good to be true. She only had to hope that this wasn't some kind of sign they were going to bounce back in difficult ways

She supposed, at least, it would be a break from the melancholy routine she'd seemed to have fallen into. Something different, in any case.

\#

"No, seriously, this is my treat. You've already fed me baked goods twice."

Marigold reluctantly put away her card, and Laurel ordered for them both, while Marigold grabbed a seat by the window. Laurel carried over their slices of cake and the table number for coffees. She smiled despite herself, seeing Marigold sitting there, her chin on her hand, smiling too, as if to herself – as if unaware of the world.

"Hey," said Laurel, sitting down, feeling a little awkward.

Marigold stretched up. "Hi! Your hair looks awesome."

"Thank you." Laurel had done a long herbal wash to make the blue more vivid last night. She knew people got the sense there was something different, but she hadn't had anyone observant enough to comment on it changing her hair specifically. Marigold was clearly observant.

"Sorry, I say what I think sometimes. Sometimes it works out well for me. Sometimes not so much."

"You don't need to apologise. How is your day going?"

Marigold stretched again. "I've been at uni all day. Taught a tutorial this morning, did a lot of paperwork, submitted a grant application. So, this is clearly the interesting part of the day."

Laurel cut into her lemon cake. "I will try and live up to your expectations."

"Okay, so..." Marigold swallowed a bite of pecan pie. "You've heard a lot about what I do. You're a witch and a linguist and a barista? Tell me more!"

"Hmm, well," Laurel said, trying to find a path through all these aspects of her identity, which she simultaneously didn't really feel she lived up to at all. "I come from a witching family, not just a witching family but one with *lots* of witches. So, it was really very normal for me, growing up as a witch, which I know isn't everyone's story. We all used to mess around as kids, finding our powers, learning to use them, getting into scrapes when we got things wrong."

Laurel had been a bit of a chaos-child like everyone in her family, coming home with torn clothes and shoes full of mud or sand. But looking back, it felt like she'd also been a bit on the sidelines of it all, edging carefully, hedging her bets, never quite going all in. She noticed Marigold smiling.

"You too?"

"Ha, only child, one cousin much older than me. I spent most of my holidays drawing increasingly complicated patterns on the beach. I liked it. It was almost meditative. But I think I'd have liked to run wild occasionally too. Did you grow up in Wellington?"

Laurel shook her head. "I was born here but we moved around a bit. I spent most of my teens on the West Coast, though. How about you?"

Marigold scrunched up her nose, and Laurel found it hard not to find it cute.

"We were always sort of based here. Like, I'd always say I was from Wellington, but we lived overseas a lot. My grandmother was always here. My parents split when I was a baby, and she moved up to Hawkes Bay. Dad owned this architecture consultancy, but after I was born, he went more into teaching and lecturing and writing books about it. So that took him all over the world; six months here, then back to Wellington for a year, then another year somewhere else. Sometimes I went with him, sometimes I stayed with my grandmother, sometimes went up to Mum's."

"So you've been to heaps of places?"

"Mmm. Yes. It was sort of just my normal." Marigold polished off the last few crumbs of her cake.

"I've only ever been as far as Melbourne."

"Melbourne." Marigold pointed with her finger to emphasise the point. "I love the markets. All the spices!"

"I liked the baked goods. And the cheese."

"Those too. Those too."

They both laughed.

"How did you get started with learning about monsters?" Laurel asked.

"I had one under my bed as a kid. At my mum's place in Napier. I wasn't there a lot of the time – I mostly lived with my dad – but when I did, we'd talk 'til late. I hardly got any reading done. She's still there, I visit sometimes. I spent the summer I was eighteen there, before I went to uni, and that was when she – the monster – told me about how she felt stalled, and fearful, because even though monsters lived a long time, when they started dying no-one could help them. I had no clue what I was going to do about it, but I said I would try and help."

Later, when the two of them had said their goodbyes, and Marigold had headed down to the bus stop, Laurel walked home, stopping at the dairy on the way. She thought about what she had learned about Marigold's family. Magic was both inherited and learned, changing as it went through the generations, but there were no more witches in the Nightfield family. It seemed a shame, when Laurel's family were so widespread, in so many different fields. And yet, Marigold herself was vibrant and focused, where Laurel felt herself to be flat and indecisive.

Laurel had got two responses to her question about the Nightfield family on the witch chat. The first, from her cousin, Mildred, just said she'd heard of them before and thought they'd been in Wellington a long time. The second was more interesting. It came from a man she hadn't seen in a while. He was technically her uncle, but she mostly just called everyone a cousin at this point. He suggested she look into Bartholomew Nightfield, around the 1870s – said he'd been involved in something dodgy. He said no more, and Laurel knew she wouldn't get anything else of substance from him. A simple Google yielded nothing, so she made a note to research properly.

She stretched out on her bed. She'd enjoyed her – was it a date? she wasn't sure – with Marigold. The conversation had flowed easily, and she hadn't needed to either hide being a witch nor deal with someone's fascinated questions into it. That always made her feel like some kind of creature on display. And she had... struggled to take her eyes off

Marigold. Yeah, she'd been here before. There was really no denying how she was feeling. What she didn't know – what caused her worry – was whether Marigold felt the same way. And it was here the doubt started. What if she had got it all wrong? What if Marigold was just being polite, or friendly? What if she was just a weird creature who was like this with everyone? What if she was more interested in witchery than in Laurel herself?

Laurel tried to stop the rush of questions. If things continued like this, she'd have to get Connor to laugh at her inner monologue until it shut up. She was still a little annoyed with Connor for not only sending someone her way without asking first, but for not explaining stuff to that poor guy, and having him think she was dealing prescription drugs. Even if he *had* bought her a whole replacement bottle of vodka to make up for it, when she'd only told him he owed a koha. It was time to distract herself. Time for some baking.

#

Laurel began her research the next morning, lying on her bed with her laptop, and a chocolate coconut brownie – a product of last night's baking session – in her hand. She heard Alfred rumbling around below her; a comforting sound, a sign that all was normal.

She'd already done some quick searching and found not very much at all, except for a couple of paywalled genealogy sites which seemed to only give birth records and such like. Not of very much help, even if it was the same guy, which seemed likely. In her experience, when a witch married, the family tended to keep their surname, irrespective of gender. It meant witching family names were kept within a fairly tight-knit group, so far as extended families went.

The initial lack of results didn't discourage Laurel. She'd done a few history papers at undergrad level – enough to have looked at the national library resources before. Enough to know there were searchable scans of old newspapers, and that those newspapers included more than just the celebrities of the day. If Bartholomew Nightfield had done something significant, it was likely there in some form, even if it was filtered through the understanding of non-witches, who often came up with extremely convoluted explanations for what could be very simply explained if it was only commonly accepted that magic was a real thing.

She did a quick search for Bartholomew Nightfield and was surprised to find hundreds of results. She hoped he wasn't some kind of career criminal, up on new charges every few weeks, trying to break out of jail or something. Not that she would have objected to a criminal ancestor personally, not unless they did something truly horrible, but it was hard to guess how Marigold would have felt about it.

A quick look, though, calmed her earlier worries. Bartholomew appeared to have been a shop witch, of sorts, and most of the references to his name were essentially repetitions, variations on the same small advert for his store. They were worded in a way that may look innocent to the average person, but any witch would instantly recognise as magical supplies. Laurel set the search to exclude a couple of words from the ad and reduced the results to an entirely more manageable number.

She found an article that was altogether more interesting. An article that hinted at witchcraft.

Laurel's research was interrupted by a text from Marigold.

>> *Hey, I think someone was prowling around my house just before. Any chatter in the witch community? I reckon they were some sort of magic folk.*

>> *I'll ask the cousins. You ok?*

>> *Yeah. Thanks. Just seems dodgy.*

>> *So, y'know when I went to your house, and I felt ill? I think there's something really powerful in there. What's next to the kitchen?*

>> *That was where my grandmother lived. Sort of semi self-contained unit?*

>> *And her stuff is still there?*

>> *Most of it, yes. You think she had something?*

>> *I'm not sure exactly. But I think we should investigate. Want me to come round?*

>> *Only if it won't make you ill.*

>> *It's okay. I'll do some protection magic first.*

>> *Can I order you an Uber?*

>> *Please! In half an hour?*

>> *Will do! Thank you!*

#

Like any young witch, Laurel had been taught the basics of protection. If this was serious, she'd see a specialist – fortunately, she had two in the family – but there was no time for that now, so she simply told herself she would be fine and this really was no big deal. She messaged the cousins – she swore she'd contacted them more in this month than in the whole year preceding – and then started getting ready. First, she fastened a protection amulet around her neck. To anyone else, it would look like a plain locket, but she felt its power immediately, warm around her neck. She always carried another amulet on her keys, but this one was much stronger, and only for when she needed extra protection.

There were consequences for using more magic than needed, something she'd had drummed into her from when she was tiny.

Making a proper potion would take her hours, but she could do enough in the time she had. She started with some Angelica powder, which she mixed with black pepper. Next, she took six pieces of bamboo from her cupboard and a lump of quartz. She arranged the bamboo in a hexagon around her and sprinkled over the spices. Then she sat in the circle with the quartz, warm to the touch, and felt its energy pulse through her. She recited a spell, words she'd learned a long time ago, and then focused on their power. Magic began to build.

She focused harder, until she felt the powder being drawn to her, and the magic working its way through her. She kept her focus, until she heard the bamboo piling up in front of her. She opened her eyes. The pepper and angelica were gone. Laurel put the quartz in her pocket and felt its energy warm against her skin, even through the cloth of her trousers. She was ready.

Marigold met her outside the house, and, after a quick greeting, they headed straight in. She could feel the energy before they went through the door, and more in the living room. As she had hoped, though, what she experienced was unpleasant but not nearly as overwhelming as last time. Like music played uncomfortably loud. Part of it was the protection magic she'd done, but most of it was simply being prepared. Marigold opened the internal door, and Laurel steeled herself as the sound – or whatever it was – got louder.

The unit – a bedroom with an ensuite, a small sitting room and a kitchenette – was an odd combination of modern architecture and old-fashioned witchery. A wooden bookcase against one wall revealed many familiar leather-bound volumes, and some far rarer. The bedroom was almost empty – a made bed with a Russian Blue cat comfortably asleep on top of it, and a wardrobe which, at first glance, showed only clothes. The bathroom had clearly been cleaned out. Likewise, the kitchenette had long had the food removed from it, leaving only a few utensils and dishes in the unit under the microwave. What immediately caught Laurel's interest was in the living room. A small, glass-topped cabinet showcased pieces of delicate metalwork on its shelves. To the untrained eye, it would look like jewellery – beautiful jewellery but nothing more. Laurel knew better.

"Can I," she asked, and Marigold nodded. Laurel felt like she was trusted.

Laurel held each piece in her hand in turn, both to examine them but also because she wanted to see if she could read any traces of the now pervasive sensation as coming directly from them. They were intricately made, with patterns she knew carried magic, patterns that were older than anyone knew. Just from holding them, she had a sense of their metals; mostly silver, but there was definitely some gold, copper, and even iron in some of them. Some were visibly a mixture, two colours twisted together, others had a core of a different metal. No other material, though, no gemstones or organic material hidden inside. This was a witch who was very specific in her craft.

These weren't simple protection amulets like the one Laurel wore around her neck. These were much rarer, much more complex, and in many cases much more powerful. Laurel didn't have the knowledge to unpick exactly what they did, nor the sensitivity to know it magically – only someone who had dedicated a lot of time to working with metal would be able to do that – but she got some glimmers. Influence – even power – protection, and self-assuredness. Bending of luck and love. Marigold knew a lot about the witching world, that was for certain, but Laurel suspected she didn't know just how much power there was in this cabinet. And these items weren't even the strongest in the room.

"Your grandmother was a metal witch?" Laurel asked, although she already knew the answer.

"Yes. The third generation of them in our family, in fact. She worked on things like this, developing her magic and her craft, from when she was very young. When she stopped being able to do the heavy work, she switched to wire jewellery, but in her last years her arthritis was too bad. She dictated a book on the subject, which I'm transcribing. "

"That's so cool," Laurel said and meant it. She'd never met a witch expert in this particular discipline before. "This work is beautiful. Can I read the book?"

"Sure, when I'm done. Or I can send you the audio files."

"I'd love that," said Laurel, forcing herself to try and make conversation normally, however difficult that was with sound and vibration cascading all around. Having investigated the obvious items in the room, she moved to focus on trying to pinpoint where whatever she was having such a strong reaction to was coming from. She realised the wall next to her, between the bedroom and the living room, didn't go up to the top of the ceiling. She raised an eyebrow at Marigold.

"It's to promote flow," she said.

Laurel had been raised in dusty houses with mazes of tiny rooms. Flow sounded like a very fancy word for cold draughts. But now wasn't the time for architectural questions. She moved back and forth, pausing, closing her eyes at intervals. Getting closer, getting a clearer sense.

She thought for a moment. "Marigold, do you have something I can stand on?"

"Sure, one moment."

Marigold dragged through a stool from the breakfast bar, and Laurel climbed up, stretching enough to reach to the top of the wall. She found it easily – a loose bit of wood, a rectangle about 5 cm long and not much more than 1cm wide. She pushed down at one end until it popped up, and passed it down to Marigold. Then she felt for what was in the hollow below it. Its power threatened to overwhelm her, to throw her back from the stool and bring her crashing down against the wall. She focused on the protection she had, and the magic deep within her mind. She grounded herself, and threw the package – wrapped in some sort of soft paper – down onto the bed.

"Well, I think we've found it," she said, putting the piece of wood back in place and jumping down from the stool.

"What is it?" Marigold asked. "Shall I unwrap it."

Laurel nodded, still feeling a little dazed. She perched on the stool, while Marigold carefully unwrapped the tissue to reveal an intricately carved object. It wasn't obviously jewellery, but it could perhaps have been a brooch or pendant with the correct findings added. It was roughly circular, intricately patterned with symbols in rows leading to the centre. It reminded Laurel of some kind of flower. Whatever it was, she hadn't seen anything like it before, and Marigold confirmed she also had no knowledge of it.

"Was climbing up and down, hiding things in the tops of walls, the sort of thing your grandmother did?" Laurel asked.

Marigold shrugged. "I mean, she did surprising things. Not normally, but if she had a good enough reason she could probably have found a way. Is that still bothering you?"

Laurel nodded. "Yeah. I can cope, but..."

"One minute." Marigold scampered off into the house. Laurel could hear her footsteps heading upstairs and then back down again. She had a metal box in her hand, and she put the item – whatever it was – into it and closed the lid. "Better?"

"Much better actually. What did you do?"

"It's just an old cash box," said Marigold. "Nothing special. But I thought metal might shield the effects of metal, and that seems to be right."

Laurel breathed deeply. She hadn't realised how much the sensation had been bothering her, until it stopped, and even though she still detected a background hum, it still seemed like an unnatural silence. She steadied herself. That was one good thing at least. But they still had to work something out. And Laurel knew someone who would know.

"So, I don't know what this is," she said. "But my Aunt Penelope in the Wairarapa would be able to tell us. I've got the day off on Monday – fancy a trip?"

"Sure. At least two people owe me when it comes to covering tutes. I'll sort it."

"I'll check the trains... you don't drive, do you?"

"No," said Marigold. "But I have my dad's car if you do."

#

The road over the Remutakas clung to the sides of the hills. It was a cold day and there was snow on the top of the range. Laurel drove carefully in case of ice, bringing the car slowly around every bend, winding up and then down the hills, until at last the Wairarapa was laid out before them, vineyards and fields and then the shores of the lake. It felt good to get out of the city, if only for a few hours.

Penelope wasn't a witch, though, as a member of Laurel's family, she had a level of affinity for magical ability, even if she couldn't retain it herself. What she was, was an archivist. She'd worked in the public service in records and archives almost her entire adult life, before retiring a couple of years ago. But on the side, she'd compiled records of witchcraft. Types of magic, and its users. Magical objects. She couldn't use an item like the one Laurel and Marigold had found, but if anyone had seen anything like it before, or even just some of the markings on it; if anyone knew about anything similar, and could look up that information, it was Aunt Penelope.

"Music?" Laurel asked.

"I only like weird electronic stuff and old school punk. You should probably pick."

"What's weird electronic...?"

"You'll regret this," Marigold replied, but Laurel could see she already had Spotify open. "Alright. Here we go."

The music began with gentle piano. Laurel wasn't quite expecting that, and a few of the combinations of notes seemed a bit off, but she could live with it. And then there was a buzzing in the background, something between cicadas and static on an old fashioned car radio, that turned into a sort of clicking. It grew, until it overwhelmed the piano and then, and then everything got terribly weird.

And that was only the first minute or so, and that was the best Laurel would have been able to describe it, anyway. It mostly defied words entirely.

"What," said Laurel, twisting the steering wheel to navigate a tight bend. "The fuck. Is that?"

"It's called 'Tree Eater' and it's by Isqa."

"Not the information I was asking for, but okay. Can we have some of your old school punk now?"

Marigold's selections were maybe not Laurel's taste, but at least they sounded like music played on instruments, rather than cats having a chainsaw party. As they left the Remutaka Range behind, endless flat land spread out before them, and Laurel relaxed, untensing her shoulders. She took the roads into the Wairarapa easily, heading out towards Carterton, passing by fields of corn and vineyards, the morning sun overhead. It felt almost like a holiday – and in some ways for Laurel, it served the same purpose. It was, at least, a break in the monotony, something to shake off the routine of her life, get some different scenery and different air, and to see someone she knew outside her usual circle.

She looked over slightly, still keeping her eye on the road, and saw Marigold with her eyes closed, the breeze in her face, and her legs stretched out in front of her. The afternoon sun was golden across the young woman's skin, a slight smile on her face. All Laurel wanted to do was to stop and stare at that face.

She forced her attention back to the road.

"I can tell when you're looking at me, you know?" Marigold teased, opening her eyes and stretching.

Laurel felt herself blush, felt it creeping up across her cheeks. "Just keeping aware of my environment," she said, not looking at Marigold, and Marigold giggled briefly.

Laurel watched the land grow dusky purple and green in the afternoon winter sun. There was a glow despite the August cold. Spring didn't seem too far away – the days were getting noticeably longer now, and it felt like all kinds of possibilities were not too far over the horizons.

Laurel looked at Marigold again. If Marigold did know she was being watched, she said nothing.

#

Aunt Penelope had a lifestyle block just outside Carterton. Laurel could see it before the house; the goat wandering around, the chickens, and the vegetable plantings. Then they dipped down over the brow of the little hill and the house was on the right; about the size of Laurel's flat, but much nicer, and of course there was only one person (if you didn't count the dog and two cats, not to mention the outside animals) living there.

"Quiet out here," said Laurel, pulling up into the driveway.

"I like quiet until I don't," said Marigold. "There's been too much time alone and inside recently, and it gets too much. But sometimes I like it. I like living alone like I do now, setting my own schedule, being able to do things when and where I like and not having to stick to mealtimes and stuff."

"Cereal for dinner?" Laurel asked.

Marigold offered up her hand as a hi-five. "Cereal for dinner."

Laurel returned the gesture.

"Shall we go inside then?" she asked.

It had been a year or two since Laurel had seen Aunt Penelope. She reckoned the time had mostly gotten away from her – that and having so much family to keep in touch with – despite the two of them not really living so far from each other. She knocked on the door.

Penelope was a bit formal, and not instantly warm, but Laurel knew this was just her demeanour. Her handknitted jumper was baggy but well made, and the frames of her glasses reflected purple in the light. Marigold and Laurel slipped off their shoes at the door and followed Penelope into a room on the right, which, though probably intended as a bedroom, had been set up as a library. Built-in shelves covered every wall, breaking only for the door and windows. In the centre was a round table with four chairs.

"You girls have a seat," Penelope said. "And I'll get you some food. Is elderflower cordial good?"

"It's great," said Laurel, already basking in the comforts of witch family hospitality. She was expecting food with a lot of herbs, and sure enough the platter Penelope returned with, after bringing through the bottle of cordial and a jug of water to serve it with, was no disappointment. Homemade bread with rosemary and sea salt on top. Basil pesto – also homemade, and white bean and parsley spread. Gouda with cumin seeds, which wasn't homemade but still tasted delicious. Handfuls of nuts – pine nuts and candied almonds – and some dried fruit. This – this! – was what Laurel missed, being away from most of her family. The company as well as the food, she mentally added, spreading pesto on a piece of bread and eating hungrily, while Marigold went for the bean spread.

Penelope sat down with them, a mug of tea in her hand, cutting herself some cheese.

"You're a Nightfield," she said, pointedly looking at Marigold.

"Yes."

"Related to June?"

"She was my grandmother."

"Ah, so I knew your... your great uncle, I expect he was. June's brother in law, your grandfather's brother. Was sad to lose him."

"I was just a small child then," said Marigold. "I don't remember him but my grandfather always had his photo. I'd have liked to have known him."

"There are many regrets we all have. Still, I'm glad to see you. That's what we can do, really, keep in touch with the family we still have."

Laurel wasn't quite sure if that was an attempt to comfort Marigold or a reproach aimed at her. Or maybe Penelope was just being philosophical. In any case, it was a good opening.

"We're sort of here about Marigold's grandmother today. Or about something we believe she had in her possession."

"Oh? June was a metal witch, have I remembered that correctly?"

Marigold nodded. "Yes, that's right."

"I'm sorry she passed. It's hard – you know, I'm getting to the age where I get invited to more funerals than weddings. It can seem so much sometimes. She was very talented, from what I remember."

"She was," replied Marigold. "She was a wonderful grand-mother too."

"You're not a witch, though?"

"I'm a scientist. I do biology and genetics."

"Ah, a discipline not as far from witchcraft as many would have us believe. We work with patterns for things, often ones that don't look anything like what is created by them. Potions. Spells. Incantations. DNA is another of those in many ways."

Marigold grinned. Laurel could hear her kicking her legs back and forth under the table, something she'd noticed Marigold always did when she was happy.

"So," said Aunt Penelope. "Let's see what you've brought."

Marigold took the cash box out of her bag and opened it. Laurel bit down on her lip. She had protection spells in place, even if she was reasonably convinced it wasn't actually dangerous to her, but having it back out of metal again was still uncomfortable. Aunt Penelope showed no sign of being affected, so it really was either just Laurel or just witches.

\#

Penelope spent a long time looking at the object, taking out a magnifying glass to inspect it in close detail, and then looking in books and databases. Marigold and Laurel sat in almost reverent silence through all of this, sipping on their elderflower cordial and nibbling on the last of the cheese, almost scared to say anything, to break the silence – or Penelope's concentration. The room was dark, shaded from the sun – it had probably been a deliberate choice to store the books here – and yet at the same time it was dry. The smell of old books, behind that of the food, was a comforting one. There were further scents of herbs from the hallway.

Laurel didn't have any particular powers of smell, but she'd spent so long learning the basics of herbalism that detecting even the faintest hint of something in the background had become second nature to her. Penelope looked up, taking her glasses off and folding them back into their case.

"You were right to think of it in terms of amulets," she said, eventually. "But that's not exactly what it is. An amulet is... it's a charm, essentially. It is embodied with a particular type of magic – usually either luck or protection – and it retains that, a sort of charge if you will. If it is well made, it will allow the holder a small amount of that magic as needed. This is a bit different from that. I think I'd call it a vessel, for want of a more specific term. It's not a particular spell or charm, but a whole body of magic. A life's work, one might say, all their magical ability, but also all their magical learning and skills, developed over the course of decades, all packaged and channelled into this. Doing so would leave them powerless and would only be done when they are dying. Even then, few witches would consider doing anything of the sort. Few witches would have the ability, in any case."

"You think it's Marigold's grandmother's magic?" Laurel asked.

Penelope shook her head slowly. "I'm not certain," she said, turning the item over in her hands. "But I think it's older than that."

"Ancient..." Marigold breathed, almost inaudibly.

Penelope chuckled. "No, not ancient. Probably late nineteenth century, at a guess, though you'd need to consult a time-sensitive witch to be sure. Shame your cousin whatshisname is in Greece, Laurel, you could have asked him. In any case, it's older than your grandmother would have been, Marigold. Might have been from an older relative or someone else she knew – anyone come to mind?"

"No. But there were a lot of witches in my family, once."

"Hmm... Now there's something else – Laurel, your reaction is very strong. It *is* strong magic, but I'm surprised you were experiencing it quite as much as you were. I'd be interested to see if another witch has the same experience that you do. There's nothing else been going on for you, has there Laurel? You haven't been sick or experimenting with strong magic or something?"

Laurel shook her head. "No strong magic at all. Just a little of the usual herbalism and such like. All very basic stuff. And I've been feeling a bit under the weather, but I think I'm just sick of my job."

"Hmm," Penelope said again. "Hmm... No, none of that would account for it – though as your aunt I do feel obliged to say that maybe finishing your study would make you happier."

"I will," Laurel said, not at all sure it would ever happen, but it was the sort of thing you said to a concerned aunt. Reassured them.

"Well, I'm going to look into this more for both of you. In the meantime, keep it safe and keep yourselves safe. Got it?"

Laurel and Marigold drove back to Wellington as the light was dying, the hills purple in the late sun, and around the harbour with the water reflecting the last of the light. Laurel drove back to Marigold's home and caught the bus back into town, then walked home. She thought about some likely long-dead witch's magic, contained in a vessel and about the complex biological secrets monsters held being unravelled from tiny samples of tissue. Ways in which some aspects of people could exist outside the person, could linger long after they were gone.

It had been an illuminating day, but she still had many questions that needed answers. Who had been prowling around Marigold's house? Where had the metal object come from? And what had Marigold's grandmother been planning to use it for?

All questions she hoped would be resolved without too much drama in the coming days. Though she was beginning to realise that *without drama* was often a vain thing to hope for.

#

Laurel sat over her coffee and inhaled. She had worked every day in the past ten, some of them late shifts, some early, and twice all the way through from opening to closing, which was unreasonable in anyone's book. She'd been missing Marigold the whole time, texting her every time she got a breather. It hadn't been enough. Her sleep had been suffering. She'd kept all the questions Aunt Penelope had left her with in the back of her mind, but never really had the brain space – even when she'd had the time – to properly devote to them.

Not for the first time, Laurel felt as if she had not fully grown into her identity as a witch. She may be able to do some useful things now, but she was so aware of her limitations. She was also aware that this was only temporary; that she had no specialisation and after this, she'd go back to making the same basic potions and little else. She wasn't sure how much she'd see of Marigold then either. She wanted to solve this, but at the same time, she really didn't want things to end.

She was working later today, but for now she had a bit of time to herself. Her flatmates were at work, or up at uni, and it was just her, Tibbs, and her succulents. She opened her laptop and brought up the website of a witch-owned garden centre in Whanganui. Even though what she was ordering was from their mundane section, and not their less advertised magical section, witches still bought from witches by default. She looked through their succulent range, and picked a few: an Echeveria whose rosette pattern of light purple leaves looked almost like a flower, the colour of lavender, and a Kangaroo Paw, a plant with brilliant flame-red flowers at the top of long dark green stems.

After a second thought, she added some pots and a pack of water-holding crystals to her order, along with a new – and better – set of secateurs, as hers were getting blunted but weren't good enough quality to waste the money on having them sharpened. It all went on the credit card. It wasn't money she had easily available, but she'd picked up a couple of extra shifts this month, so she'd be able to pay it off when it was due.

She loved getting new arrivals of succulents; felt like Christmas. They'd be at her door before long, and soon it would be spring and she'd be able to start taking cuttings and passing on succulents to her friends, something she loved doing. And growing new ones for herself as well, because even those that were grown from a cutting looked somehow unique, yet at the same time, it was like watching an old friend growing to be the person – or the plant – they were meant to be.

She had been merely adequate at growing other plants, at least by witching standards. She could keep her potted herbs relatively healthy, but when she was a kid and she and her siblings had each had a plot of the garden, hers was always the least impressive. There was bush backing onto the house and she preferred to run around there. They trapped predators and were starting to remove the non-native plants, planting native ones in their place, bit by bit helping native bush to reclaim the area. Laurel was always better at laying traps and chopping things down than she was at growing things.

But when she'd started keeping succulents – the first one, a gift, and then she'd bought another, and then she'd started taking cuttings and growing them herself – came naturally. They grew perfectly. And, pleased at her success, she read everything she could, learned more, and they grew even better. She wasn't sure why, but it was a much-needed achievement in what often felt to her like a life of failure.

But at the moment, her mind had been taken over by things other than succulents. Her plants could only provide a temporary distraction. And not just the ordinary mundanities of life and work and avoiding study either. The good part of it, the happy part of it, was thinking about Marigold. She had the sense that there was something weird, something unknown, something powerful, and possibly even something dangerous going on with the item they had found in Marigold's grandmother's wall. The fact that there were people out there who were displaying a rather suspicious interest in it, well, that was less pleasant to think about, and yet it gave her a break from the mundanity of every day. In a way, it meant there was excitement among the routine of home and work, of endless flat whites and wiping tables, and walking the same route from the valley to the cafe and back.

#

For now, there was research to do. Laurel had followed her cousin's suggestion and found a record of a Bartholomew Nightfield. She still hadn't told Marigold about this research, which felt a bit weird, but she wanted to make sure there was something worth telling first.

Bartholomew Nightfield arrived in Auckland in 1875 on a ship called the Alumbagh, and turned up in Wellington a few years later. As per the adverts, he had run a haberdashery. Laurel googled that. Things used in sewing, buttons and so on. She made herself a hot chocolate and looked closer at the adverts. He was definitely selling more than buttons – the insistency on naming the metal of each type of pins in every advert: copper pins, silver pins, tin pins, and the mention of plants for sale, probably wouldn't ping anyone else's brain as being any more than a slightly unfocused shop with a shopkeeper who didn't have a knack for the concise.

For any newly arrived witch, though, those served as a sure sign that, even if they didn't already recognise the old witching family name, this was not only a place that sold witching ingredients and necessities, but a place where they would be welcome and could be put in touch with others.

It was surprisingly easy for Laurel to put together a line of descent from Bartholomew through to Marigold – or perhaps not surprisingly. Genealogies are important to witches, witching family names passed on. Most families, at least in Laurel's experience, tended to prefer to hide in plain sight rather than go off the radar. To keep everything above board with the authorities, knowing that even minor mistakes could be seized upon by someone with a grudge.

The chart Laurel put together yielded the name of another witching family. And then there was Bartholomew's daughter-in-law – Marigold's great-great-grandmother: Clara Oleander. Marigold hadn't heard of that surname before, but it sure as hell sounded witchy to her. A poisonous plant surname, just like her own.

Marigold appeared to be directly descended from not one, but three witching lines. Exactly the sort of family you would expect to have some strong magic hidden away among a deceased grandmother's possessions. Though that scenario brought to mind more an old wooden house, and a dusty attic, than it did the modernist or postmodernist – Laurel didn't know the terminology – structure of glass and concrete with a compartment dug out of the top of a wall.

So, that was one thing – who were the Oleanders? But there was another. Laurel went back to her original findings about Bartholomew. The shop adverts. He listed the same items but rotated the order each time. That made sense – seasons changed, fashions changed, and maybe he was doing what Connor called A/B marketing, trying different things and seeing how well they worked, and refining one's process accordingly. But there was something not quite right.

She kept coming back to the prices, written in the old pre-decimal money. The same numbers kept coming up, but for different items; and half the pricing made no sense. Why would you sell blue ribbons by the inch but yellow by the yard? Needles by the hundred but pins priced individually?

Laurel's witchy sense was working hard. Something wasn't right here. What if he was sending messages? What if he was using some kind of code?

Laurel grabbed her laptop, created a spreadsheet, and started to input the items: buttons, needles, ribbons, pins, even corset boning. She made separate columns for pounds, shillings, and pence, looking up the notation to make sure she got each number in the right place. How anyone calculated anything with this system, she had no idea.

Laurel sighed, pulling the laptop out from behind Tibbs.

"You're a familiar. You're supposed to aid my magic not stand in the way of it. I know cats as familiars are traditional, but sometimes I wish I'd ended up with any other creature. None could be more inconvenient than a cat."

Tibbs meowed at her and started licking his paw. Laurel rested the notepad lightly on top of the cat, as if by way of revenge, and focused on it again. There was a pattern in there, but there was too much data to see it.

Connor would be able to help her with that... but so, she guessed, could Marigold. And it was probably time to bring this all to her.

\#

"You basically wrote the code already," Marigold said, typing.

Laurel scrunched up her nose. "Really?" she said, in disbelief.

"I mean, yeah. You've done the hard part breaking it down. All I'm doing is adding syntax to it.... Right, let's give this a try."

The script outputted an error.

"Fucking semicolons," Marigold muttered. "Okay, take two."

Laurel looked at the output.

"So these are the most frequent items to be in ads, in order of frequency?"

"The most common combinations rather than items."

"I'm not seeing anything, are you? I mean, I don't know much about haberdashery a hundred years ago but…"

"It seems pretty normal to me."

Laurel thought for a moment, then brought up the newspaper site again. "Where's the one with the engagement announcement in… here. Okay, this is the announcement between Bartholomew's son and Clara Oleander, and then if we go to the shop announcement on the day…"

"Well, that's weird," Marigold said, her eyes shifting between the output on her computer and the old newspaper ad. "Most of those things on the list never appeared in another item. Indigo ribbons, massive packs buttons – massive! – copper pins…"

"It's a combination!" Laurel said, suddenly. "For a combination lock like on our family spellbook. You have to recite the numbers in your mind and it adjusts."

"And the numbers are the prices?"

"No, look. It's a whatsit. An acrostic. See, they all begin with I or M or C or L or X. It's in roman numerals. Two witching families had joined, they were locking things with a new combination, and this copy of the paper would be carried – perhaps used to line a package sent overseas – so if some harm came to that branch of the family, others they trusted would be able to access it."

"Seems a bit risky. If we could work it out..."

"Yes, but. They'd have to get their hands on the objects first."

"You think there was a spellbook in my family like yours?"

"Or maybe..." Laurel put the vessel in Marigold's hand. "Hold your fingers along the edge and think these numbers, think them until you feel numbers you can turn..."

Marigold did as Laurel suggested. "I can only feel the detailed metalwork; nothing changed." You're the witch," she said. "You try."

"Are you sure?" Laurel asked, feeling like she was intruding on Marigold's family, something she had no right to be part of in any way.

"Of course. Go on. I want to see what happens."

Slowly, carefully, Laurel removed her protection spells. The sound of the vessel became overwhelming. She bit her lip and tried to ignore it. She reached out and clutched it in her hand. Slowly her fingers found the numbers and turned the lock. The vessel was warm in her hands, and she could feel magic flowing from it, flowing from it to her, flowing through her veins sometimes smooth and warm like honey, sometimes sharp and spikey and painful. Still it kept going. She clutched the vessel hard, against her natural instinct to let it go. She looked down and saw it glowing in her hand, a golden light between each of her fingers. Marigold was watching with concern but didn't say anything.

The magic kept flowing, faster, faster, faster...

"No, no enough!" Laurel yelled, surprised by the force of her own emotion. Everything was unbearable. She pushed the vessel away across the table, Marigold catching it before it could fall. It stopped glowing when it left her hands.

Laurel felt like the room was spinning around her. Then everything turned black.

#

When she came round she was stretched out on the sofa. Her head hurt.

"What happened?" she asked

"I took your blood pressure. It went super low. That will be why you fainted."

"Uh..." said Laurel, who was not motivated to ask why Marigold had the equipment to test it just lying around in the house. She tried to sit up, but she felt dizzy. And something else...

"Here. Some water. And don't try to stand up just yet."

Laurel felt different. It wasn't just her head, or just feeling unwell. She struggled to work out what it was, struggled to work out what was going on. She could just sense the vessel, but it was like it was far in the distance. She asked Marigold if she'd taken it away.

"No, it's there on the shelf. Do you want me to move it?"

"No... I just... it's not affecting me as much. I think the magic that was in it..." She paused, hesitated for a bit. She felt something powerful deep inside her. Flows of energy coursing through her that felt both stronger and more complex than any magic she'd used before, spreading out to wrap around the gaps in her body, curling around her ribs, spreading out into the edges of her fingers...

"Marigold," she said, cautiously, and her voice came out as little more than a squeak. "Uh, I think I have new magic powers. Different ones. Ones that belonged to someone else. Maybe a long time ago. I don't know."

Marigold stretched up, suddenly seeming tall as if every muscle in her body had snapped into place. Laurel looked up at her, the serious look on her face, the curve of her cheeks, her round ears and near-shaved head.

"Laurel," said Marigold breathlessly. "You know what this means?"

Laurel shook her head, confused.

Marigold bounced onto an armchair. "I've read about this – it's super rare. It means you're a storage witch! That's why you couldn't work out what your speciality was."

"That means what? I can squeeze the shit in people's garages into half the space? Magically sort things into plastic boxes?"

Marigold laughed. "No. It means you can store things others can't. Other people's magical abilities. Their memories. If you can develop it right, it will make you really powerful. Let me find you the book I read about it in. I think they officially call it a reserve witch. I'm not surprised you haven't heard of it because it's not common at all."

Laurel hesitated, trying to find something at the edge of her memory. Something where she had got a hint of where her abilities were and then dismissed it, because she couldn't find the way down the path herself, and she didn't understand it enough to ask someone to help her. This was where she felt like she was different from everyone around her, whose talents and specialisations were becoming clear.

There was clarity even for those who weren't witches but chose, in some way, to still be part of magical communities. The ones for whom magic informed their life path and their career, even if their ability to use it themselves was limited to the little basic herbalism that almost everyone could manage with enough focus and practice, and someone to guide them.

The memory was there, just out of reach...

"I think it's why you have such an affinity for succulents, as well," Marigold said thoughtfully. "They store water until they need it. I think the world's going to need more people like you. People who can keep things alive until they are needed."

Suddenly, Laurel felt like everything was slotting into place. Years of searching, of going down the wrong tracks because most of her cousin's specialisations were something they were good at, a creative activity. It hadn't occurred to her that hers might be different, might be something more nebulous, something that would take a different process to unlock. Now, so many experiences had greater meaning, as if they had all been pointing her here, and she'd had no idea. A vague memory suddenly came into focus. She must have been four years old or thereabouts – it was certainly before she started school – and her uncle – her great uncle, to talk on technicalities – had collapsed at a barbeque. She'd been the first to get to him, screaming for help, and in between everything, just before the adults got there, just before the ambulance was called, she had put her hand on him and felt a twinge of his magic in the way she had never felt the magic of another before.

She'd known, even then, though she didn't understand what it meant, that his life was leaving his body. Then there'd been sirens and adults pulling her to one side, and shielding her from it. He lived, as it happened, another fifteen years, after some extremely complex-sounding heart surgery. And Laurel had buried most of the memory away, and certainly not processed what had happened, or why she had felt his magic.

She knew now, and she wondered if he knew all along. He was on the verge of transferring all his magic to her.

She had always been what Marigold, not very elegantly, called a Storage Witch.

#

"Do you think there's still magic in it?" Marigold asked, when she had made them corn on toast and Laurel had forced herself to eat even though she felt nauseous.

"I know there is," Laurel said. "But I think it's mostly base level magic. It's like I started at the end of a witch's life and got it working backwards. I think what's left – I don't know how I know this, I really don't – but I think what's left is stuff I can do already, mostly. Basic spells and potions.

Marigold was clearing away their plates, and Laurel was just about to ask her if she thought she should take the last of the magic from the amulet, when they heard banging and scratching noises from downstairs. Marigold looked at a tablet mounted on the wall – which Laurel quickly realised was connected to some kind of surveillance camera.

"Is this what you heard before?" she asked Marigold.

Marigold nodded.

"Looks like some monsters are paying you a visit this time."

The noises became louder, more aggressive. Marigold put a kitchen knife in her pocket. They opened the door.

The first monster was about the height of a tall human, covered in what Laurel thought was turquoise fur, but, as she looked closer, it became increasingly clear it was thousands of tiny feathers. A small mouth revealed sharp, razor-like teeth, and they had sharp, talon-like claws on each of their six paws. The other one was larger and smooth-skinned, dark green in colour, which shone as it turned in the light. They walked on four stumpy legs, with horns that curved back above their head. Their mouth was huge, stretching back almost halfway around their head in a maniacal sort of grin.

For the first time, Laurel felt rather uneasy about Alfred living beneath her floorboards.

That, however, was a matter for another day. Right now they had two very pissed-off monsters... large monsters with claws and teeth.

The green monster bared their teeth and growled.

Even for Laurel, who had happily lived with a monster a long time, that was a warning sign. Monsters weren't any more likely to be malevolent or violent than humans were – probably less so. But on the occasions they got nasty, they had the potential to do serious damage. She did not like being on the wrong side of them.

Marigold made a noise that appeared to be speaking to the monsters, terribly politely. The turquoise monster responded – not in words, but by attempting to swipe her face with their outstretched talons. They missed, only as Marigold ducked.

Laurel ran, and tried to pull Marigold away, but she refused to move more than a couple of metres around the side of the house, yelling something back at the monster as she did.

"They want the vessel?" Laurel asked, feeling her heart speed up, too scared to look at the monsters heading towards them both.

"I think it's my samples. We can't let them get them. I..."

Laurel looked up, and she saw the green monster, its sharp horns and its grin. She knew they didn't stand a chance here. She saw Marigold and knew she couldn't leave her.

"Please, you can replace..." She tugged at Marigold's sleeve, but there was little more important to Marigold than her research – and certainly not her own life. She was stronger than she looked and wasn't going anywhere.

Laurel felt something impossible growing inside her, something powerful, something she could not contain.

"Please, Marigold," she said, and Marigold... turned and ran with her, across the road, their footsteps together, keeping ahead.

"I don't..." Marigold didn't finish, but Laurel understood. She had made Marigold run. She should not have that level of power and yet...

Yet, there were more pressing things at hand, as they slowed and caught their breath.

"What do they want with your samples?" Laurel asked.

"I'm trying..." Marigold breathed. "I'm trying to explain it to them. But it's hard. I don't know the words in their language and they won't listen."

"Explain what?"

"I think they don't understand I just have cellular samples. They think I'm keeping monsters captive."

The monsters were gaining on them, angry. Even though Laurel had no idea how to interpret their facial expressions, she could still see the fury in their eyes.

Laurel thought quickly, her footsteps still going across the tarmac, and down the steep hill, so fast she wasn't sure she could have stopped even had she wanted to. She couldn't fight them alone. But she wasn't alone. She had all the magic of a witch from a century ago... and she had Marigold. She had Marigold...

Laurel gripped the vessel in her pocket in one hand. With the other, she grabbed Marigold's arm and took a deep breath. She felt the magic flow from the object into her and then through to Marigold. Everything felt warm and alive, like she was a mere part of something much bigger, something that had begun long before she was born, and would continue long after she was gone. It flamed in her, brighter than anything, and then, just as suddenly, died to an ember. Laurel breathed, deeply. The experience was at once magical – invigorating – and exhausting. She felt more alive than she had ever been, and she felt exhausted all at the same time.

She understood, at least on a basic level, what she'd done. She'd transferred the remaining magic from the vessel, what had been left from when she'd collapsed, and passed it on to Marigold. A witch's early life, her spells and experimentation, the first flickers of magic from a young witch long ago. But those words in no way captured the enormity of the experience.

She could have kept going, given her more of what she had taken earlier – and it would have been a relief to do so because she felt, even now, the bubbling pressure of so much magic inside of her, the tension in her head and underneath her skin. But she released her grip. For all Laurel's relative inexperience and lack of specialisation, she knew she could handle it. Marigold was an unknown quantity in this regard.

Laurel opened her eyes.

Marigold grinned. "I think we didn't work out the half of it." She took the amulet from Laurel.

Laurel offered no resistance. It was clear Marigold was meant to have it. Laurel had played her part; now it was Marigold's turn.

Laurel watched as metal worked its way out. Wires un-curled and unfurled like tentacles, spreading out around Marigold's fingers, encircling her body not as a cage but as if Marigold was just at the centre of a growing plant. Branches and roots spread everywhere, growing and unfurling and working their way outwards, curling around fences and mailboxes and trees.

Marigold's eyes glowed blue-green, glowed with power. The metal looked like it was burning white-hot, and yet Marigold showed no sign of pain as she held it in her palm. She raised it up above her head and where the wires should have snagged and tangled they worked perfectly together, weaving their way in and out of each other to rise up with Marigold's hand.

Marigold was magic. Marigold was glowing, Marigold was filled with energy, Marigold was on fire.

Marigold was something she'd never believed she would be, and yet in some ways perhaps what she was always meant to be all at once.

And Laurel was in awe!

...and possibly a little in love.

The turquoise monster ran towards Marigold, all its legs going at once, until it seemed like it had a lot more than six, like it was some kind of brightly coloured feathered centipede. Marigold whipped the metal around. It glowed like it had just come from a furnace, white-hot and yet still not molten. It curled around as Marigold concentrated very hard. It seemed to grapple with the monster's feathers, winding its way through the monster's thick plume, and wrestling it to the ground. Then Marigold lifted the monster, throwing it over the fence, and down the bush-filled slope, where they tumbled, rolling, scattering feathers as they were snagged by plants on the way down. There was a thud and a low roar when it reached the bottom, and then it slowly began to make its way back up.

The wires snapped back into the object, or they faded into nothing, Laurel wasn't quite sure which, and Marigold looked normal again, if tired and a little dazed. She leaned over the white barrier, ready to act if the monster dared to come close again.

But the other was charging now, spirals of shades of green colours having an almost psychedelic effect. The ringed markings on its horns started to spin until Laurel felt dizzy, and then it was coming straight towards her, a massive mound of moving flesh. Marigold couldn't fight this one – she was too busy with the other. It was Laurel's turn. Marigold might be working by pure instinct, but Laurel had years of learning and practising as a witch. It didn't matter that she didn't have a specialisation, didn't matter that she was still young, and not as learned as some. She still had the ability to think back through years of after school learning, the informal classes her extended family and other witching locals – not to mention the occasional visitor or traveller – had given her. They didn't just learn about being witches. They learned about other things most people didn't believe in or chose not to see.

Think, Laurel, think, she said desperately to herself. You know this. What do you know about monsters?

She saw photocopies of writings in cursive scroll before her eyes. She could almost taste the scent of her cousin's kitchen, and freshly mown grass outside. Memories untangled. A neighbour angry, drunk, hammering on the door, threatening. A spell cast to freeze him until he calmed.

There was no chance to gather ingredients; the spell would have to stand alone with no potion to accompany it. That made it harder, but it didn't make it impossible. It was a matter of focus. Of bringing all her senses, all the different workings of her brain together. People thought magic was in the ingredients, in the substances, and maybe it was a little, but they had never been the point for Laurel. The magic was in her, and she just needed to draw it out.

She closed her eyes, focused and began the incantation. Sparks spluttered from her hands – a good start but far from enough. They came unevenly and cold, then stopped as soon as they started. She had to do better than this. She let herself relax, let herself fall into a semi-trance, blocking out everything. Now the words came more easily, flowing like poetry, like a well-learned song, or a lullaby. She didn't stop. Her hands were glowing with warmth, flushed, but she ignored them, ignored everything except her spell.

Around her, Marigold was desperately fighting with the turquoise monster and Laurel was terrified for her, but she had to put that out of her mind entirely. She had to focus, focus, focus...

She held out her hands and the air sparkled golden, like a person she'd forgotten she knew she was, like powers she'd had hidden forever.

She spoke the words out loud. She spoke them clearly, like she didn't care who heard, and she knew she had all the power she needed.

#

Laurel had more magic than she had ever known, and perhaps more than at any time before in her life. Laurel knew that now was the time she needed to use it.

Laurel flung herself around and grabbed the turquoise monster, planting her hand deep in the fur on its neck. She turned it around, using force that came from her hands, yes, but they alone were not enough to control a monster this size. She had to use something more. She had to use her magic.

But just as she did so, the other monster was running back towards the house, pausing before it. Rather than heading in at the front door, it was making its way down the side pathway to the semi-basement, scratching with great claws, claws that cut into the wood, against the door that led to Marigold's lab. Laurel looked from one direction to the other, unsure whether to try and tackle either monster or to run the hell away. Marigold had her hands over her ears, as the scratching got louder. It *was* an awful sound, but Laurel needed the use of both her hands right now...

"Freeze," she said. The monster paused, suspended in time.

It didn't last. Laurel thought she caught a flash of something in the monster's so-un-human-expression that made sense to her. It wasn't anger, and it wasn't exactly fear; it was more akin to... desperation. The monster rushed forward behind them, and Laurel grabbed Marigold's hand, realising they could not stop them, only move to one side to avoid being clawed or trampled to death.

"They really think there are monsters in here," Marigold said, horrified. "I can tell. They're like an animal fearing for its young."

Laurel wouldn't have been able to tell, but suddenly it all made sense. At that point, the monster finally broke through the door and Marigold ran after it. Laurel, against her better judgement, felt as if she had no choice but to follow.

"I asked all the monsters first," Marigold said, desperately, as they reached the door of the lab. "But I didn't think... I didn't think about if other monsters would have opinions on it. I didn't even know they detect each other. I'm used to thinking of them as being such individuals, both genetically and in their temperament..."

The turquoise monster was going for her lab equipment, for her samples. "I don't think I can replace that, if the monster..." Marigold said, distraught.

Laurel held her back. "It *is* replaceable," she said. "We'll find a way. *You're* not."

The monster went through the samples and through the equipment – carelessly, yes, and definitely clumsily, but Laurel didn't think there was really any deliberate destruction involved. She kept her hand on Marigold. She was tearful now, and clearly wanted to go rushing towards them, no doubt intending to launch into incomprehensible scientific explanations.

Then, suddenly, everything seemed to calm. The monster shook his head, and Laurel took a step back.

The monsters walked away.

#

Marigold grabbed two pods from beside the huge coffee machine, and made a drink for Laurel and then one for herself. The machine was almost as big as the one at the café. Just the thought of pods would make her boss, and half her customers, quiver, but for Laurel, any coffee she didn't have to make herself was a good coffee.

Laurel sat on a sofa without arms, which seemed to swallow her up in the middle, and felt like every muscle she possessed was on fire. She couldn't get up even if she wanted to.

"Thanks," she said, as Marigold passed her a plain, but undoubtedly expensive mug. Marigold made her own drink and then perched on one of the barstools by the breakfast bar.

"I'm glad we didn't need to kill anyone," said Marigold, reaching for a biscuit tin – or more accurately a large mason jar full of cookies. "I haven't killed anyone before, and I've been preparing in case I need to all my life, so I think I will have to one day. But I'm glad it wasn't today."

"Preparing because... monsters?" Laurel asked, bemused, sipping at her coffee.

"Not really. More just, there are a lot of possible scenarios in which it can come up. I know I have a privileged life, which makes it less likely, but there are so many things that are just down to random chance. I think today was more about misunderstandings than anything else though. A weird confluence of coincidences."

"It must have seemed to them like you had several dozen monsters trapped in your house."

"Exactly. While monsters are solitary creatures – almost by definition – they occasionally have contact with one or two others, like these two, working together in pairs. But more than a couple in a building, that's horrifying to them and clearly not a voluntary situation. So they were showing up to try and rescue others of their kind..."

Laurel nodded.

"...and when they got here, they found, or they detected, the magic, and assumed they were connected even though they weren't. As if it was a magic spell holding the monsters here. Which does make sense, from their point of view. I mean, if you thought someone was holding people captive in their house, you'd be pretty upset with them."

"People or monsters," said Laurel. "Though the solution would probably be different, I guess."

Laurel still felt a bit dazed from everything that had happened. She longed to return to normality... but she suspected her normality would be at least somewhat changed for the foreseeable.

"I'm sorry," she said at last. "For controlling you."

"Ah. I didn't just imagine it!"

Laurel shook her head. "I didn't know I could do it 'til it happened. I've always had the power of suggestion, been able to nudge people into thinking differently. I don't even use that, except on the landlord, because it makes me really uncomfortable."

Marigold took a sip from her mug. "Well, you probably saved me. But please, don't do it again. I know I make ridiculous decisions a lot, but I'm pretty good at looking out for myself."

"I know. I won't."

"Did it come from the vessel?"

"I'm assuming so. I mean, it's not the first time I've felt that strongly about something, and that's all it really started with, so it must be entirely new."

"Rather you with that than me, to be honest. It feels like a lot of responsibility."

"It's odd. I don't want it, and I sure as hell need to make sure I have control over using it, so I don't do that again. But I feel like all these things are coming together. Like, I know more about myself now. Or who I'm meant to be."

"This whole thing's been a set of coincidences," said Marigold. "Like if you hadn't been there, we wouldn't have known about what was hidden in the wall. I was probably expected to find it, but not quite this soon, and if I hadn't come looking for samples from Albert, you'd never have ended up at my place at all. Well... I guess it's not a coincidence for a witch to live in a house with a monster."

"It wasn't. They hoped I'd take care of him. He doesn't need much taking care of, though. As long as no-one freaks out, he seems happy enough. The cat's way more bother than he is, but that's cats for you."

"Tibbs was the real monster all along?"

They both laughed.

"He's just always there. Watching. Judging. Hungry."

"Sounds pretty much just like a regular cat to me," Marigold pointed out, turning her gaze to where the two Russian Blues had gathered by their breakfast bowls in anticipation.

"He'll be around as long as I'm around. Which is a comfort. But I swear he gets grumpier and more judgemental the older he gets. I hate to think what he'll be like in a decade, much less five."

"Ah. Well, the one thing we know about monsters is how individual they are. Maybe he'll surprise you."

Laurel laughed nervously. "I wonder how many people saw any of what went on."

"I'll put something online to say we're shooting a movie. If anyone looks it up, and tries to work out why there were a couple of monsters and something weird going on with metal on a Wilton Street, they'll find that. And sure there'll always be someone who doesn't believe it, but if there's a plausible – even semi-plausible – explanation out there that doesn't involve magic, most people are going to go with that. They always do."

Laurel nodded. "It's weird, really! So many people hoping there's magic in the world, but when they see the evidence, most of them dismiss it or explain it away because it doesn't quite fit into their world view."

"Plus, I think most of them want to believe in magic but not in monsters. Which is a shame really. Monsters are cool."

"Even though one almost clawed you to death?"

Marigold shrugged. "They had their reasons."

#

Laurel didn't sleep that night. She sat out on a dining chair in the little brick area of the garden with an insulated mug of tea, as the light grew dim, and stayed there through the cold darkness. Dawn came earlier than expected, with the sun rising in a low glow above the hills, and then gradually brightening enough that shadows fell. The past few weeks had been something of a blur, Laurel's life upended in ways she couldn't have expected when she heard that knock on the door. It seemed like an age ago.

And yet it was all still here: her flat with the monster snoring or quietly growling under the floorboards, her job that maybe wasn't that bad at all compared to some she'd had, and two of the easiest flatmates to live with. She had history and family, and she had plants and magic, her little – but comprehensive – herb garden. She could make potions when needed; she could be useful to people other than herself. Maybe the main changes in her life were to add more, not take anything away, now everything was settling down, now no monsters were sniffing around, now the issues had been resolved, and Marigold was back with her samples and her microscope and her DNA extraction equipment, and Laurel was back with her plants.

Her new succulents had arrived by courier, and she'd added them to the top of the bookcase, swapping everything around again to ensure it got enough sunlight. She'd love to be able to live somewhere that caught the sun, somewhere she didn't need to worry about them curling up brown in this shade of the wrong side of the valley. But not only were landlords increasingly refusing to accept pets, they weren't likely to be particularly accepting of an argument that familiars aren't pets either. She couldn't imagine leaving the flat with just anyone. She'd need to know they were comfortable with Alfred, and that they wouldn't be scared by him or, worse, try to hurt him. And she didn't exactly know how to go about that, short of waiting until one of her younger cousins enrolled at Vic and having them take over the lease. You couldn't exactly put "must be comfortable with monsters" in the TradeMe ad.

And in some ways, she was happy here. She'd used her magic to make it less damp, more liveable. She got on with her flatmates. She had a fully equipped kitchen and a little herb garden in pots, and Tibbs seemed happy enough – or at least as happy as an elderly cat was ever likely to seem. She was okay here for now.

#

Laurel's head ached with pressure; heavy and pulsing under the weight of her new powers. She'd been okay until she'd tried to poke at them, tried to find the edges of what she could do. Tried to find out who she was.

She kept the lights down low. Swapped shifts and then used sick leave she didn't have. She was too tired to care about being fired. Connor – concerned – left burgers and cereal bars around her door, but she couldn't eat more than a bite.

It took days before she adjusted, and she knew she was only on the edge of what she could do; knew she was in dangerous territory. This was not something to mess with. Fortunately, she had a family full of more experienced witches she knew would help. It was time for her to stop feeling inadequate around their abilities, and ask for help in growing her own.

As soon as she felt human again, once she could open the curtains in daylight and talk to people, she messaged Marigold.

>> *I think there's research still to do.*

>> *I've been thinking the same.*

Laurel propped herself up with cushions and forced herself to ignore the now-lessened headache. She needed answers.

The answers came in newspaper articles, scans of old ink-heavy paper at the end of her search. They weren't even big scandals, in the scheme of things, not over a hundred years later. Not if you didn't know how to read between the lines.

Laurel knew how to read between the lines.

Her cousin had said Bartholomew was dodgy. Laurel knew that when Bartholomew Nightfield was accused of using his daughter in law, Clara Oleander, to influence business deals on his behalf, Clara was not – as some scandalised readers must have assumed – using her good looks, her flirtatious charm, or anything along those lines. No. Clara, who appeared to be the last of the Oleander line, had possessed, exactly as Laurel suspected, the most powerful and rarest of witch powers – the ability to manipulate minds.

Pretty much every witch had some power of suggestion. But to specialise in it, to have an ability far beyond that... that was incredibly rare. And it turned out that she'd either teamed up with her father in law, or been used by him – who could say what the truth was.

Well. That explained where Marigold's family got their money from. Not that Laurel was under any illusions that there were ethical ways of being rich, but still.

Still. She had Clara Oleander's powers now. Not her personality, dead still meant dead, but the results of her later learning, development and pruning of her power's over a long life. They'd been kept in Clara's family – perhaps waiting for the right person to attain them, or a mechanism for them to do so.

Marigold arrived with a laptop under her arm, in orange dungarees with an enamel axolotl pin on one of the straps.

"How are you doing?" she asked, sitting herself down beside Laurel and pulling out a container of spicy apple cake.

"This is excellent," Laurel replied, her mouth already full. Anything to ignore the question.

"Having a rough time with the new powers still?"

"If I keep these powers, I'm going to find someone to mentor me, so I keep control."

"*If* you keep them?"

"They're your family's, your inheritance. But they would dissipate from you, likely within a couple of years."

"Hell no, I already told you I don't want them. Nah. You're responsible and thoughtful, Laurel, I think they're better off in your hands."

It was a relief to Laurel that *someone* trusted her, even if she wasn't sure she trusted herself. But it didn't feel right.

It was the magic of a very different sort of witch, a magic that had always troubled Laurel, always sat uncomfortably with her even though she'd used it – in its mildest form – on occasion. It wasn't that it was bad magic, not exactly. People thought there were good witches and bad, those who hurt and those who cured. Perhaps there were. But in Laurel's experience most witches – like most other people – wrestled with the same ethical questions and drew their lines in different places. Some maybe at extremes, but most of them clustered roughly together.

What did exist were types of magic that were easier to misuse. Ones that were more ethically complex, needing the witch who used them to tread a far narrower line than with others, if they wanted to stay in a place where their use of magic would sit easily with their conscience.

Clara Oleander's magic would – if Laurel nurtured it – be even more expansive. She would have the ability to use mind-changing magic – not just little nudges and suggestions – but the whole thing.

But Laurel's own magic, her ability to hold the powers of any witch, was perhaps equally potent if she used it in the right (or the wrong) way. She would be able to take on any kind of magic. She could have the powers of any witch. She could bestow powers.

Anyone could do magic if they were given power – Marigold included. It would fade, though, in hours or days, maybe even in weeks. Witches were born with theirs bound to them, a power that they could nurture and draw on their whole lives. But if they were given power by someone else it faded – perhaps a little slower than in someone with no magical ability, and perhaps they could make more use of it given their ability and experience, but the same principles applied.

Unless they had Laurel's abilities. Unless they were a reserve witch, one who could take on the power of any other witch – if it was offered to them, and possibly if it was not, though Laurel had no interest in pursuing *that* particular line of thought. Things were too much as it was. The magic Laurel had was not in itself evil, but it was a type of magic that Laurel was profoundly uncomfortable with using.

It sat inside her, heavy, like blood pooling in her legs. Unpleasant, uncomfortable, and perhaps unwanted, perhaps not entirely. Certainly, Laurel wished she could have chosen a lighter and less complex form of magic to be the first one she took into her soul.

"You all good?" Laurel heard Marigold ask as if she was far away, and Laurel snapped back to Earth. "Because I've been doing some research of my own."

Laurel remembered what her mother had said: "Witches can't be choosers". She was right. The few people who knew they existed were envious of witches, and they weren't wrong exactly – Laurel loved being a witch, and wouldn't have changed it for anything. But people saw them having endless power, when in fact they had endless responsibility and obligations. Not to mention a whole series of ethical quandaries and such like, which were interesting thought experiments in her teens, but not so much these days; not when she just wanted to get on with her life. She still had all the usual things to think about, after all, and she didn't really need a whole series of witchy ethical dilemmas to add to that.

But it was what it was. She just had to work out what to do with it all.

"Show me," she said to Marigold, sitting herself up better so she could see the screen.

Marigold opened up a text editor. "So, you know how we found the most common items for sale?"

"Yeah. Couldn't see much to it."

"No. But you said it was the prices that seemed most weird to you. So, I tweaked the programme to find the most common prices. And I found these 6, all of them appeared exactly 74 times over about three and a half years. And I thought, if these are going to mean anything other than prices, let's assume a decimal system, right? Even though it wasn't. So I just put a point between pounds and shillings or shillings and pence. And I got these."

12895.985.532.114.0

"I hope those aren't supposed to mean something to me?" Laurel said, her headache getting worse again.

"The odd thing is, they did seem familiar to me, but I couldn't work out how at first. I kept trying formulae to connect them, but there's no pattern. And then I realised. The periodic table. Not the current one, but Mendeleev's would have been the one in use at the time. And he put the atomic weight down for the elements. He wasn't quite accurate, but pretty good given what he had available. Scroll down!"

128 - Te95.9 - Mo85.5 - Rb32.1- S14.0 - N

The letters fell into place instantly for Laurel.

"Monster-b. Monsterb."

"Yeah, well, I guess he couldn't line it up perfectly. And here's the other thing. When I looked back over the listings, there were a lot of adjectives for items with those prices. Not all of which made sense with the items on offer. Colours, large, small, furry, feathery..."

"So was he saying he'd seen monsters...?"

"...or could put someone in touch with one? I'm not sure. But I think I know where I get my ability to speak to monsters from."

\#

Friday. Beers were opened. Leilani was cooking stir fry and microwaving roti from the dairy, with Connor overly dramatically chopping vegetables for her. It had been a while since they'd all been home at once for dinner, their fragmented lives not often lining up. It was good to spend time with each other.

Laurel was just getting plates out when there was a knock at the door. A young man, no-one Laurel had seen before.

"Hi... uh, are you Laurel? Connor told me I could get some sage here."

Laurel eyed him suspiciously, as Connor crept away.

"What do you need sage for?"

"Uh, so it's my grandmother's birthday, and I wanted to make her favourite casserole because she can't really cook any more, but she's really fussy about the recipe, so I needed fresh sage and the supermarket only had the dried stuff, and Moore Wilson's were out, and I wouldn't care about the difference but my grandmother..."

Laurel laughed and suddenly found it hard to stop, as if the strain of the past few weeks was finally dissipating.

"You want sage... you want sage for cooking?" she asked, trying to control herself.

"I... I'm sorry. I can go now, I..."

"No, look, it's fine." She pointed over to the right. "It's in that blue pot there. Help yourself." She turned to Connor. "What the fuck, Connor? Do you think I don't get enough random visitors?"

"Just thought I'd prove to you you've always been useful."

"Great. Casserole witch at your service. Now please warm the plates, Leilani will be back any moment."

Later that evening, when they had eaten and done the dishes together, Laurel got a message from Marigold. A picture of a frog.

>> *This little guy showed up yesterday. Not just a pet, right?*

Laurel confirmed it. Not just a pet. Tibbs was lying just out of reach for patting – he liked her to stretch over and make an effort. Sometimes she gave in. She sighed and rotated around on her bed to stroke under his chin. He was a grumpy cat, but she didn't know what she'd do without a familiar.

She was glad Marigold had one too. Maybe in a few years or months, he'd just be a frog again, but for now at least...

Laurel hoped she wouldn't need too much of her new power any time soon. She had wanted more variety, more interest to her life, but this had been a bit fast-paced for her. She had some other ideas about how she could change things, start to grow herself – as a person and as a witch – feeding her power, and cultivating it without having to push its limits.

It was almost spring. The succulents would need watering soon for the first time in months. They were glowing and healthy, and Laurel was starting to have some ideas. It was what Marigold had said, about storing magic like succulents stored water. And the spell, previously, where something would appear to you in the leaf of a plant. If she took cuttings, grew succulents, watered them with potions – nothing too strong, just some general good luck or protection or harmony potions – then she could sell them. Already she could see herself at the vegetable markets, at the Newtown Fair, with a little table of pots. Most people would think it was a gimmick, but they would also find they felt happier or calmer, that things started going right for them more often. And then – perhaps subconsciously – they would recommend the succulents to their friends. Some would believe pretty much anything they were told.

Only a few would know that there was real magic behind them.

Laurel picked herself up and knocked on the door to Connor's room.

"You owe me one. Can you tell me how to sell things online please?"

#

Laurel had one last spell to do. She hadn't needed the spell to trace a witch lineage – she'd been able to do that the old-fashioned, non-magical way. But a spell to see the true nature of a power... she was going to use that in a way she didn't expect...

Except it was not the vessel's power, now. It was hers.

It took her a couple of days to find all the ingredients for the potion, and another trip to Witch Way Magical supplies. She wondered if the backroom to Bartholomew Nightfield's shop had looked anything like that. She also called in some favours from suspicious cousins.

She poured the potion over one of her largest succulents, said the spell, and thought not of her power, but of Marigold's. She pictured her tentative talks with monsters – rough, prone to misunderstanding, and yet something she had never heard of anyone else being able to do.

At first, nothing happened. Then, dark patterns started to emerge on one leaf, and then another. An old man and a monster on the other side of a leaf. Then the silhouettes changed; a woman with her hair in a bun, and the monster slightly closer. A few more people, and then a silhouette that could only have been Marigold, almost close enough to touch the monster. And then others, until a young person and a monster stood side by side.

Marigold's family and monsters, becoming slowly closer, understanding each other, through the generations.

She'd keep the other implication of what she'd seen to herself for now, though. Marigold didn't need the idea that her future was pre-determined. And besides, sometimes these things could be read in multiple ways.

As for Laurel, she needed no spell. She was a storage witch currently carrying the abilities of one who could manipulate minds. Two of the most powerful, and difficult abilities out there. She would have liked, in many ways, to be a yarn witch or a baking witch – to avoid this responsibility. But there was no avoiding to be done. Good or ill, small or world-changing, the true nature of her powers depended on her.

\#

It was a week, almost two, before Laurel and Marigold saw each other again. They'd messaged each other – most nights in fact – but everything had been overwhelming, and Laurel had honestly felt quite dazed by all that had happened. Not to mention the fact that Laurel was working, and Marigold needed to catch up on research and owed a lot of people tutorial cover in return for when they'd covered for her while the whole thing was going on.

They'd each come out of this with new powers – Marigold's were minor, but she probably had the biggest adjustment to make, going from no power to some. Laurel hadn't heard of anyone who was not a witch becoming one like this. She'd heard stories of it happening, short term powers being granted especially during a crisis, but that had always been to the detriment of the giver's own powers, representing a net loss, so it was always something done either under force or in an absolutely desperate circumstance.

Laurel... Laurel's situation was different. It was like she had a whole other set of understandings inside her, a lifetime of skill and craft and magic. She wasn't quite sure how she felt about it yet. Surprisingly, Marigold also had her doubts.

"I think your grandmother would have wanted you to have it, in some way," Laurel said.

"But I'm not... I mean, I wasn't born a witch," Marigold said, confused, as the frog crawled out of her jacket and sat on her shoulder. "There was no way I could have held that power. It would have been wasted on me. It *is* wasted on me."

Laurel wrapped string tightly around the bundle of rosemary she'd cut and tied the other end around a hook above the window so it would dry.

"I don't think it's wasted..." she said slowly, feeling her way through to an understanding as she spoke. "I think to say it's wasted would assume the only value of a body of magic like that is in keeping it the same forever, hoarding it. Maybe its longevity is in sparking someone to do something else, in giving them the ability to start something new. It's a chain reaction, full of new magic and creations, not just some artefact hidden away forever.

"How can we know?" Marigold asked. "It's not like she ever mentioned it. Not like she wrote a letter."

"We'll never know. But it makes sense to me. Maybe she was intending to tell you but estimated wrongly how much time she had left. Maybe she thought you'd figure it out when it was the right time. But even if it wasn't her intention, isn't making the most of it still honouring her memory in some way?"

"Maybe..." Marigold said slowly as if she was processing the new idea. "Maybe..."

"And this is yours again," Laurel said, handing over the vessel. "It's not powerful now, but it is a family heirloom, I guess."

Marigold traced the pattern on the metal. "I didn't realise before," she said. "The flower. It's made up of letters. An O in the middle and the Cs for the petals. CO for Clara Oleander."

Laurel jumped down from the brick deck into what passed for a garden. In reality, it was somewhere between overgrown lawn and thick bush. Laurel had thought of clearing it but had never been able to summon the energy when she knew she could be given a 90-day notice – that or the house sold – at any point. She turned to offer Marigold a hand, but she'd already jumped down behind her. They gazed out at the bush that covered the steep hillside, so close to the city and yet so much wildness surrounding them, so much that was alive, so much unknown. They weren't far from the sanctuary – at least if you were a bird, exempt from the steep and curving hill roads – and so much of the birdlife flowed over to here.

It was early spring already. They walked back and along the path. They got takeaway coffee and sat on a low wall by the park. Marigold reached up and touched an early bud on the cherry tree. It burst into blossom.

"Am I a witch now?" she asked, laughing.

"For a little," Laurel replied. "Not forever. Your powers will fade, maybe over a few months, maybe a couple of years. You can't hold them. But for now, you are."

"I should make good use of them now, then," she said, and leaned over and kissed Laurel.

When Laurel felt Marigold's lips touch hers, it was as if flowers bloomed and the sun came out all in a moment. She could feel power as their lips connected, and then it glowed through them, not an overwhelming power like Laurel had experienced not so long ago, but a warm one, something unlike what she'd felt before.

"Was that magic?" Marigold asked.

"Maybe it was just you," Laurel said, grinning.

"Maybe it was just *us*" Marigold replied. "Us witches. With the future at our feet."

First-years and Familiars

This bonus short story is set a few years before Succulents and Spells, when Laurel first arrived in Wellington. Enjoy!

Laurel Windflower arrived in the room that was to be her home for the next year, closed the door, and planted herself face down on the mattress. It had been a long drive, and it felt like she'd been waiting for this for years, perhaps for her whole life. And now she was finally here, in Wellington, she didn't feel ready.

Movement came from within her backpack, still on her back. She stretched herself up.

"Sorry Tibbs," she whispered, unzipping it. The tortoise-shell cat - old now in cat years, but not witch's familiar ones wandered out and sniffed the bed suspiciously. She took out a packet of treats from the side pocket and offered one to him.

"You were very good staying still through all those rules and the welcome stuff. I think you should go under the bed for now, and we'll work out how we're going to do things."

Tibbs looked at her - and she could swear he rolled his eyes - but he got under the bed as requested.

Laurel had heard of the difficulty of student accommodation from her older siblings and cousins. There were many rules, some inconvenient or annoying, but two posed particular difficulty for witches: no candles, no pets.

Most of her family had gone flatting from first year to avoid these complications, but the housing situation was a mess in Wellington, and she didn't really know anyone except Connor who had (erroneously) got it into his head that you have to do less cleaning if you live in student accommodation, and wouldn't even consider getting a flat with her. Besides, she had wanted the full experience. This was her life just getting started, and she wanted to embrace every minute of it.

She spun herself around in the tiny room. Sunlight pierced through between two city buildings. She'd dyed her hair blue and pink - and then spent an hour scrubbing the shower - before she left and now it twirled around her, long and bright. These walls - close enough she could almost touch both sides with her finger tips - held the promise of her new life.

"Knock knock." The door opened and her mother walked in with two plastic boxes. Laurel snapped out of her daydream.

"Oh, sorry. I'll come and help carry stuff."

"I think your father's got it under control. You just tell us where you want things because you won't have room for the boxes in here, we'll need to take them. Shall I start putting your clothes away."

Laurel nodded and turned away, suddenly, irrationally tearful. She was pretty sure that the last time her mother had put her clothes away for her she hadn't yet hit your teens. All this time it had been *do it yourself* and now...

She swallowed and surveyed the storage options. Two narrow bookcases on either side of the built in desk turned into shelves above it as well. There was a wardrobe and a dresser, and a small shelf beside her bed. It wasn't bad, considering - a pretty good use of the space. She opened the box with the all-new bedding her grandmother had bought for her as a Christmas present, and began to make the bed. Lavender sheets, and a white duvet cover with embroidered ferns - she liked it. Below the pillow she put two bags of herbs she'd prepared.

Her father carried in boxes of books and began shelving them - she'd sort out the order later. With a few art prints up, and photos on the corkboard, this was starting to look like a home of sorts. She'd see her parents for brunch in the morning, before they drove back, so there was no need for final goodbyes just yet. She sat on the bed, exhausted, hearing the bustle and chatter and movement of boxes all around her. She just wanted to be alone.

She leaned on the dresser and looked herself in the mirror. Blue hair did suit her, she felt, though she might go for a lighter shade next time.

"Laurel Windflower," she said. "You are a *witch*. You can handle a bunch of students who are probably as scared as you are."

She wasn't going to be able to make a potion - she had to rely on her own courage. She changed out of her sweat-stained clothes and into a sage coloured dress, a rose quartz pendant round her neck, headed out into the corridor and... walked into one of the strongest senses of magic she'd ever experienced. And she'd grown up in a family of witches. She looked up.

The woman was about her age - she supposed everyone was - and far taller, with wet-look dark curls, and full face make-up.

"Uh hi!" Laurel said. "I'm Laurel."

"Excuse me," was the curt response. Laurel slid over and the woman walked past her, her footsteps loud on the corridor.

It's okay Laurel, she told herself. *You don't have to be friends with everyone. She's probably just anxious as well.*

She took a breath and walked on, not entirely able to shake the fear that she might just have made an enemy out of a powerful witch. At the end, past the doors to the bedrooms and bathrooms, the corridor opened out into a small sitting area with a tiny kitchenette. Two others were seated on the sofa.

"Hi," Laurel said, waiting to be dismissed again.

"Heyyy!" they chorused, and she breathed a sigh of relief. The closer of the two, with brown skin and shoulder length black hair - Māori, Laurel assumed - got up to shake her hand, her nails painted gold. "I'm Mia. Did you just arrive?"

"Laurel. Hi. My parents were helping me unload my stuff."

"Come and join us!" The other woman was wearing jeans and a shirt from what appeared to be a school sports team. Her skin was pale, her blonde hair tied back in a ponytail, and she wore hooped earrings. "I'm Charlotte. Would you like some wine? My mother left me like three cases to help me make friends because that's how *she* makes friends, and it's actually not bad."

"Sure." Laurel sat down on one of the sofas and accepted the paper cup, unsure if she'd yet drunk enough wine in her life to assess whether any particular variety was good.

"Right, so you met Lydia, dark curly hair, tall, yeah?"

"I guess so. She didn't exactly seem pleased to see me."

"Oh don't worry about it," Charlotte said. "Everyone's a bit stressed and overwhelmed. We'll get to know each other better before long. Have you met anyone else yet?"

Laurel and Mia shook their heads.

"Is it just girls on this floor?" Mia asked.

"Yeah," Charlotte replied. "Alternating floors. But I wouldn't pay the boys much interest from what I've seen. Bit clueless, still don't know how to take care of themselves, yknow?"

"Oh I don't know. A couple of them looked okay."

"Can't say I saw anything impressive. How about you Laurel?" Charlotte asked.

Laurel took a large gulp of her wine and shook her head.

"More into girls?" Charlotte asked, and Laurel nodded, her heart thumping. Was it that easy to admit it, and difficult all at once?"

"Okay, well the girls here are way better, more mature. Um there was someone here from a group... let me find the flyer."

Charlotte leafed through a heap of paper that had already accumulated on the small table.

"Here you go," she said, handing Laurel a flyer for a queer social. "See, you even get free pizza, how good is that?"

Pretty good, Laurel thought, but not as good as the fact neither of them seem to be disassociating themselves from me. She hadn't been exactly closeted at high school, so much as refused to talk about it ever. She'd seen some older students come out and be treated okay, and others met with violence.

There were already rumours about her family - they may have been able to keep the fact they were witches private, but people knew *something* was different about them, and Laurel didn't want to take the risk. Instead she and Connor just let everyone think they were a couple, dissolving into giggles if anyone asked them outright. She wasn't unpopular, but she didn't really have other friends either. She trailed along with groups, talked with whoever was closest, and waited for her life to start.

And now it was, and it felt so normal. There were fish and chips in the meal area that night, at which Laurel met the other people on her half of the floor - those who shared the same small communal space and bathrooms. All except Lydia. There was no sign of her.

Laurel hid a piece of fish in her bag and brought it back for Tibbs. He was going to have to eat mostly dry food while they were here, so he deserved treats where she could get them. He didn't seem happy, and she wondered if she should have left him with her parents but... a witch without their familiar? It wouldn't do either of them any good.

She set up her dresser as an altar before she went to bed. Dried herbs and crystals, pictures of witching ancestors, a chain of beads her brother had given her. It was a vague altar in many ways - she didn't know what kind of witch she was yet, and so didn't have anything to reflect that, but it made her feel much more connected and at home. Then she pushed on her window. It stuck a little but opened. Just enough for a cat to get out. She looked down. There was a little ledge outside, which connected to others. It looked like Tibbs would have no problems getting onto the roof or the fire escape.

"Okay cat," she said, picking him up. I'm sorry to do this to you, but you're going to need to be out a lot of the time. Be careful - there's more traffic than you're used to. You can sleep in here but I can't risk it during the day. And don't whatever you do be seen coming in the window.

She looked round, and placed a small stack of books on the windowsill, and after a few moments he jumped onto those and then he squeezed himself through the open window, and was gone. Laurel sighed. He understood more than most cats, but he was in most ways still a cat. He knew he had to make himself scarce, but she wasn't sure if he understood why she was doing this to him. Or if he'd sympathise if he did.

She did a quick tarot reading before going to bed - a past, present, future spread, what is life going to be like for me in Wellington. She turned over the cards - The Moon. She nodded. Anxiety and what is hidden, yep, fair. Nine of cups - contentment, emotional fulfillment - she wasn't there yet, but maybe it was beginning to happen. Maybe. Then The Lovers.

She knew the lovers wasn't always literal, but her heart was thumping anyway. She was yet to go on a single date - and now there was a prospect of her finding love?

She switched off the light, and then she curled up under her new duvet, listening to the sounds from the street below through the open window. She was half asleep when she heard Tibbs come back through, and curled up by her feet, same way he always did.

She settled in okay over the next week. Endless social and introductory events kept her too busy to think too much about the initial bout of homesickness with - she supposed it was design. She discovered the little weekend market in a carpark at the end of the street where she could buy fresh herbs. She brought in cat food in a backpack which she kept hidden under the bed. She grew used to Tibbs sliding in and out, making his way deftly along ledges and pipes. She felt bad he had no place he could be secure, but it was only for eight months, and then she'd probably go back to her parents for a bit and then find a flat where pets were approved in the new year.

She joined the French club, the Latin club, the Queer social club, the tennis club. She got to know everyone on her floor, finding all of them easier to talk to than she'd assumed - all of them except Lydia.

Lydia... Laurel had never been in conflict with another witch before - it hadn't really occurred to her that she might be. Almost all the witches she'd met were family, after all. She supposed Lydia was in some way trying to distance herself from her magic, or avoid a discussion about it, but the way she looked down at Laurel, snubbed her at every opportunity, felt... unpleasant.

And the worst of it? The worst of it was that she couldn't deny that Lydia was hot - not just pretty but the sort of hot that makes you forget words in her presence. Her brain felt like it was being ripped in two; half of her knew that Lydia wasn't her friend, to try to avoid her, the other half struggled to stop looking at her

She wondered if she'd been that obvious. If *that* was the reason Lydia didn't like her. It wasn't simple homophobia, because Lydia was friends with Keira who was bi and spoke with the sort of confidence that indicated she'd been out for years, but maybe she'd realised Laurel was attracted to her and was freaked out.

She hoped not. She didn't want to be that obvious to people.

Lydia went to classes - French which she'd studied at school, and Psychology and Linguistics which she hadn't. She met classmates and she sucked in every word she was taught as if it were arcane knowledge - and maybe there was a hint of magic in it. Some people knew what form their witching powers were taking from when they were very young; that wasn't the case for Laurel, but she was assuming she would sooner or later. And maybe here, among the structure of language and its evolution, she'd find her own specialised form of magic.

Instead she found girls. She found the excitable redhead with dramatic clothing choices and a good natured but loud sense of humour in her Linguistics tutorial. She found the friendly girl with the copper-brown skin and long hair who could guide conversation perfectly in her French lectures. She played tennis with the blonde girl whose skin was so pale you could see the veins through it and had a dog she let Laurel pet when it became clear she was missing her own family's animals.

(Well most of them. She wasn't quite ready to tell her about Tibbs yet.)

Every single one of them was perfect, the one she wanted to spend every minute with, the one she started making ridiculous mistakes when she talked to them.

"It's meant to be a stereotype," she whispered to Tibbs one night. "I'm not meant to be attracted to *everybody*."

Tibbs stretched out beside her, showing his claws.

"Yes, okay, it's not everybody. But it's like 5 people at once that my face starts burning up when I get near them. Tell me the rest of my life isn't going to be like... oh hell, we got you fixed didn't we, so this is probably a bit outside your experience. Sorry about that!"

Tibbs probably wasn't the best person to confide in about this, and she'd barely seen Connor since she arrived - he'd been getting involved in some scheme or another with other students in the Compsci department. Cryptocurrency, they called it, which seemed an exciting name for what struck Laurel as a very dubious idea - .

Connor and her had always looked out for each other, but now she needed him, and he, by the sounds of it, *definitely* needed her. She burrowed her face in her pillow and did her best to sleep as Tibbs kneaded the duvet around her feet.

The second week of classes, she got an email from her Aunt Penelope, who lived in the Wairarapa but still worked in Wellington - some kind of public service job - offering to buy her lunch. She hadn't seen her aunt in a while - and her connections in the city all felt... flimsy, recently made. It would be good to have family nearby. Laurel looked at her lecture timetable, made a time, and less than a week later was happily eating chicken noodle salad and ginger slice in a Lambton Quay cafe while politely answering all the the usual questions: she was studying linguistics, her classes seemed interesting, her room was small but nice enough, she'd figured out where the markets were and how to get a library book.

"And you've discovered Witch Way, of course?"

Lauren looked blank?

"Which way?"

Penelope looked at her watch.

"I don't have to be in a meeting until two. Come on, let's go for a walk."

Aunt Penelope walked briskly up the hill with Laurel just a little behind. The daily climbs up the steps to uni had made her calves ache the first week, but she could tell she was getting stronger bit by bit. She supposed after a few months of living in Wellington she'd be zipping up and down hills as easily as on the flat. She wasn't quite there yet. They crossed the bridge over the motorway into Thorndon. Thorndon was full of bistros and boutique shops where Laurel didn't ever expect to be able to afford to shop. It was an early suburb of the city, the other side of the botanic gardens from campus.

Laurel looked around, inhaling everything. She caught a slight smell on the wind, bergamot and yarrow and... was that yellow dock. Penelope smiled at her.

"Yes. This place doesn't need a street frontage to advertise itself to witches. Come on. "

They walked round the back of an antique shop and along a little path. Chimes above the unassuming door jangled when Laurel opened it tentatively. she breathed in and felt a rush of everything she had grown up with straight to her head. This wasn't some local market where she could find the right culinary herbs if she looked hard enough; this was everything, fresh and dried; this was herbs and woods and potion-pots and feathers and frog bones and witchlights and and...

The boy behind the counter looked slightly out of place - fifteen or so in a rugby shirt, his hair untidy round his ears.

"Your father's away today?" Penelope asked him.

"He'll be back in an hour."

"Oh that's a shame - I wanted to introduce my niece to him. Anyway. Barnabas, this is Laurel, she's just started at Vic."

"And a witch?"

Laurel held out her hand. "Yes. You as well?"

"I'm a wizard," he said, picking up a cartoonishly pointy hat and mockingly putting it on his head. Despite the fooling, though, Laurel could tell he was serious about the wizard part of it.

"Wizard? Is that like... a gender thing? Because male witches in my family are just witches."

"Oh. Oh no. No if I started claiming that mum would put me on lawn mowing duty for years. It means I'm a student of magic but don't really have much innate ability. Studying it more from a theoretical point of view. I think other people use it differently, so don't take it from me - as my father likes to say, I don't know everything - but that's what I'm doing. Is there anything you need?"

Laurel looked round. "Uh, everything. I'm not sure. This place is amazing. I've had what I've grown myself and a bit ordered online before. I can't believe my parents never took me here when we visited."

"Got to leave plenty for you to discover on your own," Penelope said. Now, I need to head back to work if you want to walk with me, but now you know where this is, you'll be able to come back here. Oh and don't forget the notice board as well. That's how witches and other magic folk connect round here."

Laurel looked around. "Oh, before I go. Any treats for a cat familiar. Beyond regular cat treats, I mean. He's having a bit of a hard time..."

The boy smirked. "You mean you're hiding him in a student hostel. You're not the first, won't be the last. I've got just the thing for you..."

The knock on her door started Laurel. She'd been lying on her bed, officially studying but more accurately watching downloads of *Elementary*.

"RA. Can you let me in, please?"

Laurel's heart started before remembering that Tibbs was outside. She muttered a quick spell; *let what you seek be hidden, if finding do me ill* and hope that would be enough to disguise the cat supplies, just in case. Then she opened the door. She could never place the RA's name; white, with shoulder length brown hair and very optimistic. She supposed one had to be naturally cheery to be an RA.

"I just need to have a quick look round please?"

"Sure," Laurel said, pretending not to be nervous as the RA looked in her wardrobe, and under the bed where the cat food and other needs were stowed. She looked straight past them.

"Can I help you find something?" Laurel asked.

"A rumour going round that someone's been hiding a cat... probably just a joke, still, we've got to check. Well, no sign of anything like that in here." She straightened up and turned to look at Laurel's altar.

"Ah another pagan - there are a few of you this year. Are you aware of our rules around candles?"

Pagan wasn't exactly how Laurel would have described herself, but the sense of acceptance was a relief. She picked up one of the plastic tea lights and flicked the switch on the bottom. "Look, entirely fire safe."

"Very good. Stick to those; you do not want to be responsible for everyone freezing outside in their pyjamas at 3am, believe me."

Plastic tea lights weren't the same as real candles, of course, but half of what she did with candles was focusing on the flame, and she reckoned she could learn to do that. When she couldn't... she'd find a park or a bit of bush, somewhere she could be alone at night, and carry out her magic there.

As soon as the RA had gone, Laurel shut the window. Her heart was beating fast enough to feel it. Someone had seen Tibbs despite how careful she'd been - it was stupid of her to think she could disguise his presence for this long. She was going to have to work something else out... something else, she had family members who could take him, but not close by, and being separated from him, however grumpy, was more than being separated from a beloved pet. It was like part of herself being cut away from her.

But later, when she talked with others over breakfast the next morning, the rumour still flying thick and fast but no cat apparently found, it was quite consistent that the cat was a long haired tabby, and not her aging tortoiseshell shorthair.

Was it possible there were two cats being hidden in the hostel? Even two familiars. It would make sense; Lydia appeared to be a witch and her room was right across the corridor from Laurel's. Not all witches' familiars were cats, but it was very common.

Whether it was Tibbs who had been spotted or not, Laurel knew that she had to up her game. It was time for some more powerful magic.

The spell book she kept on her shelves wasn't the original family spell book, but her own mix of copies from the original, and some additions of her own, spells other family members had told her. In generations it might seem as hefty and mystical as the original, but for now it was a hard backed sketchbook from an art store, covered in brown paper, with spells glued in and a few handwritten notations, the occasional sticker just for the hell of it.

Potions and herbalism had always been Laure's thing. They were a bit difficult when you didn't have a kitchen to yourself, but she chose a time when most people were at lectures and made up some nonsense about natural air freshener should anyone ask. She gave the largest pot she could find a good clean, and then set it to boil with water. She added herbs from her collection, mustard seeds and willow bark, and a piece of amethyst that would be removed when she was done.

She put some in Tibbs' drinking water and sprinkled some of the rest around her room. It wouldn't make him invisible, but it would definitely make him less likely to be noticed.

Standing outside the hostel two days later, she was less than confident it had worked. Two cats now were hanging out on the front of the building, taking in the sun on two of the wider ledges. One of them was Tibbs. The other was not.

She watched the two of them silently as they so quietly made their way around, jumping between ledges and pipes and onto the fire escape. Her first thought was that Tibbs had found a friend. Then she decided that was ridiculous because Tibbs was a grumpy old cat who barely knew the meaning of friend. But something else was up.

"Tibbs," she said, under her breath. She knew he could still hear sounds that quiet, even though he pretended not to. Both cats turned to look at her, and she swore she saw alarm in her familiar's eyes. Then the tabby ran off, scampering and leaping up the windowsills to the roof and round a corner while Tibbs - slowly, deliberately - made his way down the fire escape to her.

"Who's that you're hanging with?" she said, ticking him under his chin, but the cat wasn't telling. But she knew now, knew that there definitely was another cat in the building. And surely no-one would go to the effort of hiding a regular pet. No. It had to be another witch. And she was fairly sure it was Lydia - but if she just asked she knew she'd deny it. She needed proof.

It was time for another potion. She gathered her ingredients. Rosemary for remembering where one truly belongs. Garlic - her neighbours were going to love this one - for harmony in your home, which she thought gave a reasonable chance of not having a fight with Lydia. And calendula for psychic strength.

She boiled it up on the stove, hoping no-one would ask what she was doing. It didn't really make sense to be making stock when you only had a kitchenette and all your meals were catered, so she would have had to say witchcraft, but

make them think it was some vague ritual about mindful-
ness or - worse - the law of attraction, or other concepts she
detested, rather than actual witchcraft.

It smelled right, which was a good sign, but some things
you only know until you try them. She let it cool and
then strained some into a spray bottle she'd bought for the
purpose. The rest went into an old coke bottle. She didn't
expect to need extra, or to have another use for it, but there
was no reason to waste it just now.

Now she just had to find the cat again.

Before she could deal with the cat issue, she had an appointment. An appointment she was really wishing she
hadn't made, that she was regretting even considering. But
the queer social group had said their senior members were
happy to do one on one chats and... maybe they could tell
Laurel how to shut her brain up.

"I like, haven't been disowned or harassed or anything,"
she said awkwardly, pulling up a chair as offered.

"That's okay. There's no sign on the door saying "only the people with the worst problems in the world can enter. How are things going for you."

Laurel forced a smile. "Well it's going okay, my parents are mostly okay - I think they don't know how to talk about it, but if I meet someone who fits into the family well then it will all be fine."

"And you're meeting new people here? I've seen you at some of our socials. I know they can be a bit awkward..."

"No they're good. I mean. People are nice."

"And it's the first time you've really been out."

"More or less. Just to my best friend before - we covered for each other. My parents knew, and I think a few more people guessed, but I didn't talk about it."

"So it's a bit of an adjustment then."

"Yeah." Laurel felt herself blush. "Okay, this makes me sound bad and I don't know if it's normal but I feel like I'm crushing on everyone. And I know that's a really bad stereotype, like, if someone's gay they're automatically attracted to you, but it's like everywhere I look there's someone. And I just want to be normal. Like, sometimes like a particular person. Date them. That sort of thing. Just like straight people do."

"Okay, so, first off - you don't have to fit the heterosexual norm if that's not what you want. Lots of straight people don't. There are lots of ways to organise relationships, they don't have to be monogamous, all that. I can give you some reading on that if you're interested. But, uh secondly, Laurel, and I say this kindly, *you've just come out.*"

Laurel stared at the wall, allowing herself to smile a little.

"Yeah, I guess," she said.

"Seriously. If you'd been into boys you'd have had years and years to process this and people making comments and practice and everything. Instead, what, you've been awkwardly trying to avoid looking interested in anyone, avoiding getting too close, and now suddenly you're in a new place and you can do all that stuff. Floodgates opened! *It makes perfect sense that you're crushing on every possible candidate.*"

"So it's not always going to be like this?" Laurel asked, wrapping her feet around the legs of the chair.

"My money's on the fact things will settle down for you as you get used to having options and start to get a better sense of who you find attractive and why. But yknow, if it doesn't, if you're still someone who is attracted to a lot of people well... learn to enjoy it. It's not your fault if people stereotype us."

Laurel processed the whole conversation as she walked down the steps into town and back to her room. There was a lot going on. As if uni classes, and living independently, and all this coming out stuff wasn't enough to deal with, she still had to find out who the other witch in the building was. Things just couldn't be easy, could they?

Tibbs wound his way around her ankles and walked from Laurel to the door. Laurel got the message and opened the door, poking her head out quickly to see if anyone was around. No sign. She was anxious about being caught but she knew if Tibbs was being similarly incautious then there must be a reason.

She followed him through to the communal area just in time to see a large, fluffy tabby leap down from a high window.

Laurel grabbed the spray bottle from her purse. She knew the cat would likely never forgive her, but she had to know who the other witch was, because at this point they were both putting each other in danger. She sprayed the cat with the potion and let it work its magic. She expected to see the owner of the cat beside her, or more likely a trail she could follow to them. Instead...

"Oh shit!" Laurel yelled, and turned away. She took off the shirt she was wearing over her tank top and threw it behind her. "I'll uh. Shit. I'll get a blanket."

A dash to her room and back and there was Lydia sitting on the sofa, wrapped in a blanket. Tibbs was nowhere to be found, but she'd worry about that later.

"So I guess you found my secret."

"Uh. Yeah. Not what I expected but. Yeah."

"You going to report me."

"What? No. I just thought there was another witch in the building and wanted to talk to them so our cats didn't get discovered. Are you going to report *me*?"

Laurel shook her head.

"No. Uh. So you can just shapeshift? Like turn into a cat and back again? Seriously?"

Laurel had grown up in a magical family - she really shouldn't be surprised by anything - but somehow this was something she'd never expected.

"I don't have control over when and where. It's... it's more like migraines. There are triggers I can try to avoid and sometimes I can see it coming and do my best to get in a convenient situation for it. Worst case I at least manage to hide in a bathroom or a doorway. But it's not something I can turn on and off at will. My family understand. We were all homeschooled, this little collective of my extended family and a few others. We got each other. I could have stayed there. We have a couple of family businesses so none of us have to go out into the real world but I...

"...you wanted to go to the city. You wanted to go dancing and drinking in overpriced bars and study and travel the world..."

"...yes, and I've wanted to be a lawyer since I was twelve. There was a lot of preparation - potions I can take to help me control it - and we did a lot of planning. They wanted to rent me this little cottage way over in Makara, but hell no. I wouldn't see anyone. And I know I'm taking a risk, and I know it's not just me that may have to bear the consequences..."

"I get it," Laurel said. "I get it... wait, hang on. You're from Christchurch?"

"Rural, a bit north of the city. Closer to Hamner Springs. Why?"

Laurel giggled. "So... so the Canterbury Panther is... real???"

Lydia laughed. "No of course not. But people started thinking there might be magical cats out there, and we needed to put them off the scent. So we started spreading rumours - well, my grandparents did - and before you know it every time anyone saw a larger than average black cat they were freaking out about panthers. All the weirdness got diverted to that - and no-one thought to look at a family that shifted into regular housecats and back."

"Smart."

"I like to think so. The Fjordland moose on the other hand..."

"Oh no, don't tell me they're shapeshifters as well..."

"No, regular moose, brought over from Canada or their descendents. The only fun part of the mystery is who's helping them survive... or stay hidden."

They sit in silence for a little while before Lydia speaks.

"Uh. I'm sorry for being rude to you. It's just. There are no pet rules here and I really just wanted to have a normal student experience like everyone else. You could tell something was going on with me."

"Yeah. I thought you were a witch with an attitude problem."

Lydia looked down at her hands and Laurel swore she could see her fingernails retract, just a little.

"*You* are, though? I mean a witch not..."

Laurel nodded.

"Yeah. And like with you, it runs in the family. It's, sort of a secret, sort of not. I let people think I just mess around with crystals a lot, but not that there's any actual magic involved. And I'm not very powerful and I don't specialise in anything yet, but yes, I can work magic."

"And you've been helping your cat stay hidden using magic...?"

"Well. He's a familiar so he understands more than regular cats. But yeah, I've been using magic as well."

"My family has potions but... I don't know if it's okay to ask, but maybe you can do something better? It's really important to me to be able to stay here."

Laurel's first instinct was to say yes, of course she would. But even though Lydia had apologised, she wanted to be more confident, to stand her ground.

"I'll need something in return," she says. "Not money. What can you offer?"

Lydia stifled a laugh.

"What?" Laurel asked.

"No, I just had a bad thought."

"Well you've got to tell me now."

"Uh... I was going to ask if you liked half dead birds through your window at 3am."

Laurel cracked up then.

"No. No. I would not. I already have Tibbs to contend with, who is fortunately not a hunter - I've told him if he does he's getting a clown collar with a bell. We have an understanding."

"But I was thinking. You're a witch, so you must use plants and stuff in your potions. And some of them you get from trees. Well I can climb trees, a lot more easily and discretely than most people can, so if you need me to get anything for you... I'll be a collector for your spells."

Laurel offered out her hand.

"Deal," she said. "Let's take over the kitchenette and make some potions".

It was one of the last days that felt like summer, a few days before the Easter break. Laurel joined Charlotte and Mia, a couple of the others from their group of rooms, in putting together a picnic. Many of them would be heading home for Easter - or travelling to see other relatives, or just getting out of the city. Laurel couldn't believe the first six weeks had gone by so fast.

And yet here they were in early April, sprawled out in the park under a cluster of trees, sharing bread and cheese and chocolate brownies.

"So Laurel," Mia said, grinning. "No offence or anything, but there's a rumour going round that you're a witch. Any truth to it?"

And Laurel realised that there were choices between telling everything and being scared all the time.

"I don't have a broomstick, if that's what you're asking. And I won't be turning you into a frog. But I can read tarot if you'd like."

And she took a deck out of her bag, and began to shuffle the cards.

A note from Andi R. Christopher

Hello, and thank you for reading. I wrote *Succulents and Spells* in the chaos that was early 2020, teaming up with writer friends to start a fun project to get us through the worry and the restrictions of lockdown.

At the time much of my day job was focused on ensuring disabled people had accessible information about the pandemic and I was feeling the weight of that – if anything kept me going it was the chance to write about magic and cute relationships with a group that cheered each other on. We've now released move than twenty witchy novellas by a spooky 13 authors. Please do head to witchyfiction.com and check them out – I truly believe there's something there for everyone.

This new edition of *Succulents and Spells* includes a short story set a few years before, when Laurel first arrived in Wellington. I've also brought this series to sit under my new pen name, Andi R. Christopher. Same me, just trying to keep similar books together so it's easier for you to find more of what you love. Huge thanks to Marie, Toni, Helen, Jamie and everyone else for your help and support.

The series is now complete, following Laurel and Marigold, and two other witchy couples, over five books. If you want to find out what happens next, check out Microscopes and Magic.

I've also started a new series set in Aotearoa New Zealand. It's filled with sea magic and mystery, following a young woman as she discovers her powers. It starts with Tides of Magic, available from all the usual retailers.

Lastly, I'd love to keep in touch with you via my newsletter. You can subscribe at https://andi.digitalpress.blog / And if you liked *Succulents and Spells*, please consider reviewing it on Goodreads or your ebook site of choice. Every review helps!

About the author

Andi R. Christopher is a writer of queer urban and contemporary fantasy. Their Charley Deacon series – stories of sea magic and self discovery – begins with "Tides of Magic", out now, and their previous Windflower series comprises cosy novellas about queer witches in Aotearoa New Zealand. They also write speculative fiction as Andi C. Buchanan. You can find them online at andirchristopher.com or https://linktr.ee/andiwrites.

Also by Andi R. Christopher

Windflower Series

Succulents and Spells
Microscopes and Magic
Alpaca and Apparitions
Data and Divination
Weddings and Witchcraft

Charley Deacon Series

Tides of Magic
Tides of Change